"When it comes to paranormal romance with explosive action scenes, Bradley has that nailed."

~*Entertainment Weekly*

"Action-packed, sexy, and fun! Reminiscent of J.R. Ward —but with Vikings!"

~Ilona Andrews, *New York Times* Bestselling Author

"An entertaining read when you like crime stories with a touch of paranormal and shape-shifting."

~Honest Bookworm for *Flash of Fear*

"...a swoon-worthy hero who sizzles across the pages in this tale full of passion, blood, and destiny! Sexy, stubborn, and smart lovers clash in a tension-filled race to outwit science and control fate."

~Rebecca Zanetti, *New York Times* Bestselling Author

"Bradley's story is a whirlwind of action, suspense, humor, and a ton of romance! ...you'll be reading this page-turner the whole day!"

~*Bookstr*

"Nonstop action, satisfying romantic encounters, and intriguing world building make this a thoroughly enjoyable paranormal-romance series."

~*Booklist*

"...blends Norse mythology and evil government experiments into an unusual paranormal...the immortal Viking premise is perfect for paranormal romance readers who are looking for something different."

~*Publishers Weekly*

WOLF HUNGER

NORSE WARRIOR PROTECTORS

ASA MARIA BRADLEY

WOLF HUNGER

Can an alpha wolf catch a thief who bends the laws of physics?

Wolf shifter and billionaire Arek Varg runs a security company specializing in bodyguards, extraction teams, and hostage rescue. He's also the alpha of all the Western Packs and uses his ancient Odin medallion to connect with his packs' magic and lead his wolves as a cohesive unit. With war brewing between the four major shifter coalitions, the last thing he needs is a mysterious woman stealing his relic. He'll use all of his resources to hunt her down.

And if he does, will she tame him?

Former museum curator Dr. Laney Marconi was the darling of the magical artifacts' academic world until she fell from grace due to a scandal based on false accusations. She now reclaims stolen items for insurance companies, using her witch powers that manipulate parallel dimensions. When a routine case turns into a disaster of epic proportions, she needs to evade the sexy shifter she stole from long enough to figure out who set her up.

The hunt is on.

But with Arek hot on her heels, Laney is forced to decide if salvaging the few crumbs left of her good reputation is worth teaming up with the alpha wolf whose ice-blue gaze pierces her shields while he demands nothing less than her soul.

Subscribe to my newsletter for new releases updates, bonus content, and exclusive giveaways: www.asamariabradley.com/newsletter/

This one is for Eric and Ellen. You're amazing. I'm so proud and honored to be your Auntie!

GLOSSARY

Since I am from Sweden, I use mostly that language's version of the Norse mythology terms. Also, these definitions are how they apply to the *Norse Warrior Protectors* world. Other Norse mythology sources offer different meanings

This glossary spans the entire series. Some of these terms may not appear in this book. Also, in the Scandinavian languages, the letters *Å*, *Ä* and Ö, or their equivalent, appear at the end of the alphabets. But here, I've put them at the beginning because that is where most English speakers would look for them.

Terms & Phrases

Älskling: Term of endearment. The literal translation would be something like "beloved." But it's often used as Americans use "dearest" or "darling."

Älv Förtrollning: Swedish term *for elven magic, elven illusions.*

Æsir: A family of deities concerned mainly with the cultivation of power and war.

Asgård, Asgard: The realm (world) where Gods and Goddesses live.

Battle Mark: A scar earned in battle and therefore brings the wearer honor and beauty.

Berserker: The Valkyries' and Vikings' internal warrior spirit that whips into battle fury when they—or someone they love—are threatened.

Blót: A ceremony that connects the warriors with each other and the deity to which the blót is aimed. Usually a communal toast is invoked.

Borg: Swedish term for *Fortress.*

Drottning: Swedish term for *Queen.*

Eddas: See *Icelandic Sagas.*

Einherjar: Vikings and Valkyries who died in battle and then trained with Odin and Freya in *Asgard.* When ready, the gods send them back to Midgard to protect the regular humans.

Eir: Goddess of healing. Her symbols are the mortar and pestle and she has a gray jaybird as a companion.

Feberandas: What the Vikings and Valkyries call it when they absorb human sexual emotions to keep their berserker spirits from entering permanent battle fury. Literal translation: Fever Breathing.

Folkvagn: Another word for *Freya's Meadow*. Where Valkyries who have died an honorable death spend their afterlife, training with Freya until she sends them back to Midgard to protect regular humans.

Freki: One of Odin's two wolves. They haunt the battle field and feast on the slain warrior who are not admitted to *Valhalla* or *Folkvagn*. The name means the gluttonous or greedy one.

Freya/Freyja: The goddess of fertility, sex, beauty, and war. She rides a chariot pulled by two cats that Thor gave her, and rules the Norse Gods' Council with Odin. Unlike most of the Norse Gods and Goddesses on the council, she belongs to a group of deities called Vanir that are able to see the future and practice *seidhr*.

Freya's Meadow: Where Valkyries who have died an honorable death spend their afterlife, training with Freya until she sends them back to Midgard to protect regular humans.

Frigg: Odin's wife and goddess of marriage and motherhood.

Garm: The wolfhound that guard the entrance to Hel, the underworld of the dead.

Geri: One of Odin's two wolves. They haunt the battle field and feast on the slain warrior who are not admitted to *Valhalla* or *Folkvagn*. The name means the greedy or the ravenous one.

Hel: The underworld of the dead. The entrance is guarded by the wolfhound Garm.

Honorable Death: A death earned in battle, which earns you a place in *Valhalla* or *Folkvagn*.

Huginn: One of Odin's ravens. The name means thought.

Håll tyst: Swedish for *shut up*.

Icelandic Sagas: Collective noun for the *Prose Edda* and the *Poetic Edda*, plus other texts about Norse Mythology and Viking kings. They were written in the 13th century, hundreds of years after the end of the Viking age.

Jänta: Swedish term for *little girl*.

Järv: Swedish term for *wolverine.*

Jävlar, helvetes, skit: Swedish cursing phrase. Literal translation: Devils, hells, shit.

Jörmungandr: The Midgard Serpent
A gigantic sea serpent or worm that encircles the Earth and bites its own tail. The violent unrest of the sea as the Midgard Serpent lets go of its tale is a sign of *Ragnarök* starting.

Jul: Swedish term for *Yule, Christmas.*

Julbord: A big spread of Swedish Christmas foods.

Julgåva: Swedish term for *Yule Gift, Christmas Present.*

Kung: Swedish term for *King.*

Langbardarland: What the Vikings called today's Italy.

Lofn: The goddess of forbidden love. She champions true love beyond challenges and traditional boundaries. She personifies that love in all its manifestations is sacred and worthy of divine protection.

Loki: The trickster god prophesied to instigate *Ragnarök.* He can shape shift.

Mjöd: Mead. An alcoholic drink made by fermenting honey and mixing it with water. Sometimes spices and other fruits are added.

Midgård, Midgard: The realm (world) where humans live.

Midsommar: Midsummer/Summer Solstice, a big holiday and celebration in Sweden.

Mimers Brunn/Källa: Mimi's Well
The well of wisdom that nourishes one of Yggdrasil's roots.

Min Drottning: Swedish for *My Queen*.

Min Kung: Swedish for *My King*.

Muninn: One of Odin's ravens. The name means memory.

Noita: Finnish for wise woman or witch.

Norns: Three deities responsible for shaping destiny. (Similar to the three fates in other mythologies.) They rule the threads of time and draw water from their sacred well, Wyrd, to nourish Yggdrasil. Urd (what has been) spins the threads, Verdandi (what is to be) weaves them, and Skuld (what should be) cuts them short. The Norns invented the Runes. They shape destinies by carving runes into Yggdrasil's bark.

Odin/Oden: One-eyed god of wisdom and war. He rules the Norse Gods' council with Freya. Odin sacrificed his eye for a sip from *Mimers Brunn*—the well of wisdom—to become all-knowing. Sometimes referred to as "The Wise One."

Påg: Southern Swedish term for little boy.

Pojke: Swedish term for little boy.

Ragnarök: The prophesied final battle between the Norse Gods and other mythological creatures and the end of the worlds. A great flood sweeps the realms, but two humans will survive and start a new world. Loki thinks he will be the only surviving deity and the ruler of this new world.

Runes: Old Norse alphabet and magical symbols.

Saami/Sámi: A nomadic indigenous people who live the region of Sápmi, which covers large northern parts of Norway, Sweden, Finland, and the Kola Peninsula in Russia.

Sagas: See *Icelandic Sagas*.

Seidhr: Magic associated with telling and shaping the future. The magic of the *Norns*.

Sill: Pickled herring.

Själsfrände: A Viking's or Valkyrie's soulmate. When they meet their *själsfrände*, the Midgard Serpent tattoo on their non-sword arm begins to grow and they have to complete the bond with their soulmate or succumb to permanent battle fury. If they do, Odin and Freya have to call them back to Asgard, since they'll be a danger to themselves and their battle brothers and sisters.

Skål: Swedish for cheers.

Sleipnir: Odin's eight-footed horse.

Stallare: Marshall, second in command.

Stormhatt: Monkshood or Wolfsbane, poisonous herb.

Svärd: Sword

True Mate: An ulfhednar shifter's soulmate. When they meet their true mate, they have to complete their bond or lose control over their wolf. If they do, they'll be hunted and killed by their pack since they are now a danger to themselves and other wolves.

Ulfhednar: Wolf shifters who serve as Odin's and Freya's elite warriors.

Valhalla: Odin's mead hall where warriors who died in battle spend eternity, training with Odin. Or spend as much time as they need before Odin sends them back to *Midgard* to protect regular humans.

Vanir: A group of deities who practice *seidhr,* magic associated with telling and shaping the future.

Wyrd: The Norns' sacred well.

Yggdrasil: The World Tree, The Tree of Life. A sacred ash tree that grows in the middle of *Asgard* and ties the nine realms (worlds) of Norse Mythology together.

CHAPTER 1

Leaning back against the bar of Dev Beat, a popular San Francisco nightclub, Laney Marconi tugged on the hem of her short black dress and took a sip of her club soda. She'd asked the bartender to garnish the glass with a slice of lime so that it looked like a gin and tonic. The drink and the outfit were all part of her disguise to look like a regular club patron. Blue and purple ceiling strobe lights pulsed in time with the loud music screaming from the speakers. Strategically placed Cobalt neon lights made the oval-shaped bar, and the liquor shelves in the middle look as if they were carved out of ice—a suitable environment for hunting a Swedish wolf.

Laney smiled to herself. But when a man at the bar took that as an invitation to step closer, she quickly schooled her features into her regular resting-bitch-face. With a snooty head-toss, she flipped the long red tresses of her wig over her shoulder as she dismissed the guy. Laney continued on her path around the bar, closer and closer to her target this evening, Arek Varg.

Since he wasn't looking her way, Laney took a moment to study him through a mirror on the wall opposite. She'd never met him, but his reputation made him instantly recognizable. Or maybe lack of reputation was a better expression because the head alpha of the western wolf packs kept his security locked down tight. Laney had scoured the internet for information, but Mr. Varg had no social media presence.

His company's website provided only information about their security services, nothing about its handsome owner. Arek Varg's short blond hair and azure eyes betrayed his Scandinavian origin, and the tailored cornflower-colored button-down shirt he wore deepened his eye color. A perfectly groomed beard hugged his square jaw. He looked like he should be in a movie or on a billboard.

The gossip press agreed with that assessment. Despite sparse details about his life, magazines and blogs published every photo of him they could get their hands on. His Nordic sharp looks combined with the secrecy of his life sold copies like crazy.

She kept watching Varg via the wall of mirrors as she positioned herself on the opposite side of the race-track-shaped bar from where he sat. Even though the bar staff flittered between them as they filled drink orders, she had a clear view of him. Laney felt almost voyeuristic watching him without his knowledge, but that was part of the job and when the target looked like this alpha, she didn't mind at all. He kept looking at his phone. Maybe to check the time, or perhaps he expected a message.

Laney's client had assured her that Varg would come to the bar at this precise time. She had no idea what they'd used to lure him. And she didn't care.

Her job was just to recover the stolen artifact that Varg wore around his neck. She was too far away to see the medallion details, but the pictures the client had sent showed a platinum wolf's head inscribed with runes and three interlocking triangles. At first, the wealthy shifter being her new target had surprised her. Although few details about Varg's personal life and background were public, the supernatural community knew him as being upstanding and honest, if archaic in some of his leadership actions. The only few rumblings she'd been able to dig up about the popular alpha were about members who broke pack rules and got punished a little too severely by Varg's enforcer.

But none of that was Laney's concern. The only thing she worried about was recovering the stolen talisman for the insurance company that had hired her. She may have fallen far from her former prestigious academic career, but she still prided herself on doing a job quickly and professionally. Besides, the heels she'd chosen to wear with the black dress were pinching her toes, and she wanted to get home and change her party outfit for comfy slippers and pajamas.

Time to get busy.

She slowly strode along the bar as if looking for an opening among the throng gathered at the counter so she could order another drink from the bartender.

She needed to be close enough to strike when the perfect opportunity presented itself, but not so near that she attracted Varg's attention or, goddess forbid, made eye contact. She'd learned the hard way that people better remembered individuals they'd looked in the eye, even if only for a fleeting moment. Should that happen, she relied on the wig and the black dress to disguise what she really looked like.

Five people separated them now.

Laney sipped the dregs of her drink as she again used the mirrors to monitor her mark. She tapped her toe impatiently and squelched the butterflies in her stomach. These feelings always showed up right before the action started. Nerves mixed with excitement and anticipation. Later on, back home and safe in her apartment, the adrenaline crash would exhaust her. But right now, that same adrenaline sharpened her senses and gave her hyper-focus.

It also heightened her imagination, because despite the loud music, she heard Varg's shirt rustling. The expensive fabric caressed the skin of his arm as he turned the phone to look at the display again. The impatient sigh that left his lips caressed her ears. She even felt the warmth from his body as irritation heated his blood. A flush spread across her chest and crept up her neck to bloom on her face.

Dang it! She nudged the bar with her bare leg to cool down.

Obviously, she needed to get out more. Or maybe just upgrade her vibrator. She'd been in a dry spell since her last relationship. The hurtful breakup that ended said relationship inspired her to reach for battery-operated loving whenever she craved an orgasm.

Finally, what she'd been waiting for happened.

A tall brunette in a slinky red dress that perfectly draped and displayed her curves approached Varg. The woman placed her elbow on the bar and leaned to face Varg. Hidden from the alpha's view by the woman, Laney quickly decreased the distance between them until she stood on the other side of the temptress, facing the bar. Frankly, it surprised Laney that it had taken this long for anyone to flirt with Varg. Maybe his grim expression and impatient energy kept potential hookups away.

What was the male equivalent of resting bitch face? Resting jerk face? Resting dick face?

She smiled to herself again, and the bartender interpreted that as an ask. She stepped up to Laney. "Can I get you another one?" the petite woman with bright purple hair gestured toward Laney's drink.

"Oh no, I'm fine," she answered.

The bartender quirked one lavender eyebrow but continued toward other customers who gestured for refills.

Crap, Laney had gotten caught up in her musings and the bartender's question. Rule number one, never take your eyes off the target. She angled her body so she could see Varg and the woman as they talked.

The temptress in the red dress had good game. She'd cocked a hip against the bar and flicked her thick shiny hair over one shoulder. A sultry smile played on her lips as she lowered her eyelids and traced a finger on the rim of her red wine glass.

Laney almost felt sorry for Varg or whoever did his laundry, but hopefully, the stain would come out of that beautiful shirt he wore. She quickly twisted and bumped into the brunette. As the other woman splashed the handsome wolf alpha with wine, Laney slipped around her, with Varg in her sight.

The quick burst of power channeled through her fingertips broke the medallion's chain around the alpha's neck. Laney caught the artifact and slipped it down her cleavage as she kept moving past and away from the couple.

She joined the crowd on the dance floor and moved with the music. Raising her arms to the ceiling, she closed her eyes and abandoned her body to the rhythm of the beat. Her hips swayed as she danced herself closer to the middle of the floor so that people shielded her from the soaked alpha. The medallion heated her skin as it lay nestled in nestled between her breasts. Sweat broke out on her forehead as she resisted the temptation to tap into its magic. This ancient jewelry wanted to speak to her and tell her centuries of stories.

Laney struggled against its enchanted promises of power and knowledge. She needed to transport it to a parallel dimension quickly, in case she got caught.

When she'd been Dr. Marconi in the Anthropology and Archeology department at the university, she'd used her powers over earthbound materials only to evaluate and date historical artifacts. She'd never shared how they would sometimes sing to her, nor her shifting-dimensions ability. Her colleagues would have considered both cheap party tricks, or worse, suspected her of cultivating a talent so she could steal priceless objects.

Now, quantum dimension shifting provided her a way to make a living. She refused to give in to the feeling of shame that sometimes came over her when she thought about how low she'd sunk.

Tomorrow, she'd meet with the insurance company representatives, who would then return the artifact to its rightful owner. Like many of their competitors, they'd rather hire an independent contractor to recover the items instead of calling the police. That way, they could keep news about stolen items from the press.

Returning objects to their rightful owner gave Laney a small sense of pride, but mostly she cared about the check she'd earn that would finally make it possible to pay her outstanding bills and rent.

She brought her arms down again and covered her chest with her palms as she kept dancing. She guided her power into the medallion, deeper and deeper, until the platinum metal vibrated on a molecular level. A half-second later, she felt it disappearing beyond the space she and the other dancers occupied. Its presence was still with her, but it was with a different her, another Laney. That woman danced in a club just like this one, with the artifact still nestled in her cleavage. To Laney-here-and-now, she appeared hazy, as if in a dream.

All she had to do now was maintain the connection with that other Laney until she got back to her apartment. Once there, she'd channel the medallion back to this dimension and then lock it away in the safe in her apartment.

She headed for the exit, throwing a quick glance over her shoulder. Varg gestured toward a tall man who looked like part of the club's security staff. The pretty woman sobbed into her hands.

A small stab of guilt pierced Laney's heart, but she shook it off. This was no longer her problem.

CHAPTER 2

Arek paced his office, glaring at his two closest friends, who also served as his second-in-command wolves. "How the hell could this happen?" he addressed to the room at large. He wanted to hit something, but the modern chrome and glass desk and bookcases would shatter, and he didn't feel like dealing with the mess of slivers. Why hadn't he chosen solid wood for his office furniture?

Bolt, who lazily reclined in one of the black leather visitors' opposite Arek's desk, answered. "You went out alone, again." His voice sounded calm, but his ordinarily hazel eyes were now bottle green—a sign of Bolt's alert and unhappy wolf. The unhappy part, Arek felt, even though he wasn't wearing his Odin medallion. His lieutenants were part of his pack, and as their alpha, he connected with them easily. But as the Commanding Alpha of the Western packs, he needed to tap into every pack in the coalition, and that required the Odin medallion as his focus. A detail he hadn't shared with anyone, including the men in this office.

Legend said that centuries ago, the medallion held true magic and allowed its bearer to connect with Asgard, the dwelling of the gods. Rumors about the talisman's magical properties had flown wildly for ages. The latest outrageous story Arek had heard involved him teleporting. However, the medallion served only as a symbol of Arek and his wolves serving Odin and Freya as Ulfhednar—elite soldiers who could take the shape of wolves—and it worked as a focus for pack magic. As far as he knew, none of the other alphas in the Western Packs Coalition, or any other coalition, had anything like it.

Justice occupied the other chair, and his crisp British voice drawled out, "Fuck, mate, our duty is to keep you safe and carry out your orders, but you make the job ridiculously hard with your need to be the lone wolf." His eyes momentarily flashed purple, but then Justice blinked, and they returned to his human greyish silver. That rare flash worried Arek because the man kept all his emotions bottled up. Justice had a reputation for being stone-cold in all situations. It served him well as the coalition packs' enforcer. If his wolf simmered close enough to the surface to peek out of Justice's eyes, Arek's lone jaunt to the club had pissed off his two lieutenants more than he thought.

Arek adjusted the collar of his shirt. Red wine still stained the garment, but at least it had dried now. "What the fuck was I supposed to do? You were both out, and the caller insisted we meet immediately." He knew that sounded ridiculous, but he felt a childish need to defend himself.

Worst of all, he knew Justice was right. As an alpha, he shouldn't venture out alone. It sent a message of arrogance to other wolves, or worse, showed that he didn't trust his second-in-commands. Neither was true.

Well, okay, most people would describe him as arrogant. But he definitely trusted his closest friends.

Bolt studied him with those eerie green eyes, his voice still as ever. "And you didn't think there was something off about the fact that the caller chose a nightclub as a meeting point? A place full of people, despite insisting on keeping his identity hidden and seeming to be on the run from someone?"

Fuck. Now that Bolt said it out loud, Arek could hear how stupid he'd been. "The information was important," he stupidly and immaturely defended himself again. "Too important to worry about the details of the meeting place."

Justice raised a dark eyebrow but remained quiet.

"Okay, fine, I should have waited for one of you to get back," Arek threw out. With these wolves, he could afford to lose a little face. They were his closest pack members, his brothers.

"Or at least taken one of the other wolves with you," Bolt interjected.

"Yes," Arek conceded through clenched teeth. He knew both of them were correct, but he'd wanted to go on his own to check out if the information was useful. He'd foolishly thought he could keep the meeting from Bolt if it weren't. Fuck, he was an idiot. He should have known it was a trap. And now the Odin medallion was gone. Anger flowed through his body, sharpening his senses. The wolf inside him awoke and almost purred.

The beast loved anger.

"What was this vital information?" Justice asked, his eyes glimmering purple again. This time in response to Arek's wolf coming out. As a pack member, Justice automatically responded to his alpha.

Despite the open top button, Arek's shirt felt constricted. He snapped the second open as well. It didn't help. "He said he knew where Arrow is." He avoided looking at Bolt, but out of the corner of his eye, he could see the man snapping to attention.

"What the fuck?" Bolt growled. Any mention of his twin brother pissed him off, but Arek could also sense longing and sorrow behind that anger. Not that he'd ever let Bolt know he could sense those emotions through the pack bond. His lieutenant would shut down all communication quicker than a bunny chased through a field. The estranged twins hadn't seen each other for years, but Bolt wouldn't say why. "You put yourself in danger because of Arrow, and didn't take me as backup?"

Justice held out a hand to calm the other man. "What about Arrow?"

Arek pinched the bridge of his nose. "I never found out. The caller said he knew where Arrow might be." He finally met Bolt's gaze. "I thought I'd check it out for you to see if it was legit." He shrugged apologetically. He'd tried to protect his lieutenant from any false hope. But Arrow once belonged to their pack, and therefore still counted as one of Arek's wolves. Once pack, always pack, until he formally rescinded Arek as his alpha.

Justice chimed in, "We'll figure out who set this up, mate. But right now, let's concentrate on the actual thief."

Arek nodded. "We don't have to reveal the artifact's true importance. People know the necklace belonged to my grandfather. Besides its sentimental value, as Commanding Alpha, I can't let anyone get away with stealing from me. I would lose respect." Some would consider the medallion's role in his ability to connect emotionally with packs other than his own as witchcraft. Wolves abhorred true magic, since it could manipulate them. If a witch threw a spell at them, they had to tap into the pack bonds quickly to protect themselves. But often, wolves would lose themselves to the magic before they noticed it had them trapped. Or at least that was how the stories went.

Arek didn't share the prejudice against all supernatural powers, but had collected as many magical artifacts as he could during the years he'd been a wolf. That way, they couldn't hurt him or any other shifters. "It's been less than an hour since the thief stole the medallion. We should be able to catch them, or at least identify them before morning."

Bolt growled again, but then relaxed in his seat. It appeared he'd let the issue of Arrow rest. At least for now.

"I'm already on it," Justice said, holding up a tablet. "The club sent over the security videos from the cameras covering the bar. I've isolated the one that had the best angle covering Arek's location." He reached for a remote control and aimed it at the fifty-inch flatscreen on the wall. With a click of the remote's power button and a few taps on the tablet, a grainy video feed displayed on the larger screen.

Arek watched the images of himself sitting in the bar, impatiently tapping his fingers and checking his phone. "Fast forward," he said, and Justice did as asked, but then slowed the feed to regular speed as a brown-haired woman in a red dress approached Arek on the screen.

"It took a while before any females approached you," Bolt said. "You're losing your touch."

Arek didn't bother to answer but allowed his wolf to emit a short growl.

Justice chuckled.

When Bolt joined in, Arek's shirt finally didn't feel so tight anymore.

In Norse mythology, Odin always had two loyal wolves at his side, Geri and Freki. Not that Arek compared himself to the All-Father, but he often felt like Bolt and Justice were his true loyal companions. Their wolves would stand with his, no matter the threat. Just like his would lay down its life for theirs.

Two loyal companions who didn't mind giving him shit.

They weren't wrong, though. Usually, Arek had plenty of female attention, but he didn't blame the women in the bar for not talking to him. Even on the screen, he could see a cloud of irritation and anger surrounding him. Looking at his pinched face and furrowed brow, it surprised him anyone had been brave enough to approach him.

Not only had the poor woman gotten an earful when she spilled her wine on him by accident, but she'd then had to put up with being interrogated after the medallion had disappeared. He'd been so busy wiping his shirt that he hadn't associated the slight sting on his neck with someone breaking the chain and stealing the jewelry.

Right off his fucking neck. The wolf growled again.

It hadn't taken long to figure out that the brunette wasn't in on the theft. She'd just been in the wrong place at the wrong time. Arek had apologized, but when she left, her tear-stained face showed how much she regretted hitting on him that night.

Such a shame too. She was quite attractive. Normally he'd been receptive to her flirtations, but the promised news of Arrow had distracted him.

The version of himself on the video was busy wiping off his shirt when something on the screen caught real-time Arek's eye. "Stop," he barked. "Back it up a few frames."

Justice paused the footage, and the three of them leaned closer toward the flatscreen on the wall. "What do you see?" Bolt asked.

"That woman behind the brunette," Arek said. "The one who's talking to the bartender. Her drink is almost empty, but she's not ordering another one."

"Maybe she'd had enough," Bolt suggested. "Or maybe the purple hair turned her off. I find it hot."

The hairs on the back of Arek's neck stood. "No, there's something off about how she's holding herself. She's talking to the bartender, who's standing slightly to the right of her. And yet, she's angling her face to the left."

"She's looking at you." Bolt stood and walked closer to the flatscreen. "Maybe she's wondering why you're so irritated when a gorgeous woman is trying to pick you up."

"I'm slowing down the video," Justice said. The footage displayed in slow motion as they watched the woman.

He hadn't noticed the woman while at the bar, but somehow that black dress had registered in his subconscious. Arek studied her slim, athletic build. Racking his brain to see if she looked like anyone he knew. If it were anyone who'd shared his bed, he would know the details of her body. He may offer none of his lovers' commitment, but he always took his time learning their bodies so he could find out how to please them properly. Nobody left his bed unsatisfied.

The woman had her back toward the camera and they could only see the profile of her face. She had long, red hair—his subconscious fed him that detail too—and her short black dress revealed a few enticing curves, but didn't cling tight enough to her body to garner too much attention. She'd dressed like someone who would fit in perfectly on the club scene, but not stand out. The perfect outfit for a small jewelry heist.

As they watched, the woman put her drink on the bar and slipped out of frame right when the brunette spilled her drink on Arek. "Where did she go?" he asked.

"I'm looking for her." Justice tapped furiously on the tablet. "Got her."

The flatscreen flickered, and the bar displayed from a different angle. This one from further away and higher. Part of the dance floor now showed up on the screen.

Arek watched the repeated conversation between the mystery woman in the black dress and the bartender. This time, when the woman slipped away, she still appeared in the frame. If Justice hadn't slowed down the footage's speed, Arek would have missed the woman's elbow quickly poking the back of the brunette in the red dress.

"Fuck, she pushed her," Justice said.

It looked like the mystery woman briefly touched Arek's shoulder as she slipped by him. But he knew that was the moment the medallion had disappeared. That's his neck had stung.

He rubbed the spot where she'd zapped him. What the fuck had she used? A taser? She had nothing in her hands on the screen. "She's the one who took the Odin medallion." His tone took on the darkness of the anger coursing through his veins.

Justice rewound the footage. "Are you sure? I didn't see her steal it."

"Certain," Arek answered, still staring at the screen. "Find out who she is."

"Do you know her?" Bolt asked.

"I do not," Arek answered, now sure he'd never met the woman before. "But she'll definitely get to know me." He turned to face his two lieutenants. "Find her." A grim smile curved his lips upward. "Hunt her down."

CHAPTER 3

Laney double-checked the address on the business card that Mr. Hartford gave her when she initially visited the Global Securities building to sign the contract that hired her to retrieve the magical medallion. Just like the other two times she'd looked at the little piece of stiff paper, the address was the same as when she'd met with Mr. Hartford a week ago.

On that occasion, though, the lobby's receptionist fought against a tide of phones ringing off the hook. Busy employees walked the hallways, carrying folders and speaking with each other animatedly. Furniture and computers filled glass-walled offices and actual people used those computers to work, supposedly.

That was what she realized now. Supposedly. Because now, a desolate office landscape greeted her. There were no people, no furniture, and no phones or computers. The only things showing that this once had been a busy place of business were the indentations that the desks and chairs had left on the carpet.

It was not a weekend. She'd checked.

It was not a national holiday. She'd double-checked.

Her stomach churned, and nausea rose in the back of her throat. She'd been duped.

But by whom? Did Varg and his pack get to Global Securities?

She'd walked into the building just like last time, not really noticing, but now thought twice about the absent security guard on the entrance floor. She'd taken the elevator to the tenth floor of the building, just like she did her previous visit.

Maybe the company had gone bankrupt. It felt weird hoping for the demise of her client, but the alternatives were too frightening.

She pulled out her phone and called the number on Mr. Hartford's business card, hoping a would ring from an office somewhere on the floor. If it did, it would be a phantom phone.

She'd already checked them all. They were all empty. Signal after signal echoed down the phone line as she waited for someone to answer.

Nobody did.

After a while, her phone disconnected the call automatically.

Refusing to acknowledge what was slowly becoming painfully clear, she stubbornly hit redial—with the same result.

Her knees gave out, and she sunk to the floor. Tears welled in her eyes.

This was bad on so many levels.

If this insurance company was fake, the mission had been fake, which meant she'd just stolen a magical artifact from the Commanding Alpha of the Western Packs.

If Varg and his wolves had been here, they'd be watching for her and storm the building any minute.

Laney rubbed her forehead and willed her tears to stop.

Think. Think hard.

She'd been here long enough for the pack to rush in. They hadn't, yet, so chance were they were not who had made an entire company disappear.

The logical answer—or more like illogical—was that her client had duped her. She'd dwell on why later. Right now, her brain could only focus on one thing at a time. Too many of its cells were firing neurons in a blind panic and not fit for rational thoughts.

Could she return the medallion to Varg before he found her? Her body shuddered at the thought. For reasons she didn't want to examine too closely—see, panicked brain cells—she did not want to encounter the alpha up close, especially if he was angry.

Especially if she'd caused that anger.

"What the hell do I do now?" she wondered out loud.

Maybe she could turn the medallion into the police and say she'd found it.

She dismissed the idea, shuddering as she remembered how much havoc a magical item could wreak if in regular human hands, or even worse, a person who had power but didn't know how to use it.

Like when the regular-human-led archaeological dig in Italy had discovered a powerful ancient Christian relic a few decades back. The baptismal font looked like any other old stone basin but had harnessed magic. A lot of magic.

The archaeologists placed the find in a monastery church close to the dig site. Unfortunately, a nun of the order who worshipped in the church had a tiny trickle of power in her blood. During prayer, she uttered a Latin scripture that had the exact wording necessary to awaken the magic within the ancient baptismal font.

It had filled with water and kept on filling until it overflowed the church, the monastery, the village, and the surrounding countryside. Witches and mages from several universities had to combine their powers to stop the water. The mainstream media had reported the incident as a freak flash flood. But among magic practitioners, it became a case study for why gifted humans shouldn't meddle with magic.

Now, university departments, such as the one Laney had belonged to, kept track of all archeological findings, just in case some possessed power, sleeping or not.

Thinking about her past life, when she'd been a darling of the witches and mages' academic world, always hurt. Laney quickly ordered her functional brain cells away from that.

She continued speaking out loud to herself, "Could construct some sort of box to return the item. One that dampens the powers or shields it?"

"That's a great idea. Unfortunately, you will not have the chance to try that out," a heavily accented Russian voice said.

Laney's head snapped up.

A man entirely dressed in black stood before her.

She jumped to her feet, stumbling backward. How had she not heard anyone approaching?

Then the stench of dark magic reached her nose, and she knew he must have cloaked himself.

"Who are you?" Her voice held steady, but her insides shook. Dark magic required a blood sacrifice, and from the heavy stench surrounding the man, she suspected he'd done several.

Chills raced up her spine. She thought she'd been in trouble before, with a pissed-off alpha wolf looking for her. If dark magic practitioners were involved, she was infinitely more screwed.

The man smiled, but it didn't reach his eyes. They were so dark that Laney couldn't tell where his pupil ended and the iris started. "One of your old acquaintances, in need of help." His face blurred and kept rearranging itself. Other than the obsidian eyes, she couldn't clearly focus on his features.

She'd never be able to describe him to anyone. The magic cloaking was as effective as if he'd worn a mask, but much more menacing.

He seemed the type who enjoyed being menacing, even if it required more energy than just pulling on a piece of cloth.

And she could see why.

Not being able to focus on his face freaked out Laney's senses, increasing her nausea. The only thing she could tell for sure was that someone had broken his nose. No matter which shapes the face shifted between, the nose remained crooked.

She took a step back. "I have never met you before, and I don't see how I can help you." Brave words for a terrified woman, but she refused to show her fear.

"You already have." The man took a step closer. He moved with the fluid grace of a shifter, but he didn't give off a shifter vibe. Maybe he'd cloaked that too.

The panicked cells took control of her brain and Laney scrambled further back. "Get away from me." So much for not showing how scared she was.

The man's outline shimmered, and Mr. Hartford stood in front of her.

She gasped and tried to swallow the sound while also pushing down the big lump of dread lodged in her throat. The result came out as an undignified gulp and a quick little burp.

His kind brown eyes twinkled as he looked at her. "I'm hurt you don't recognize me, Dr. Marconi. I so enjoyed our previous conversation," Mr. Hartford said in his generic American accent. His body shimmered again, and his voice changed into the one with a Russian accent. The black-clad man stood in front of her again. "And I will enjoy our future...conversations."

The pause made Laney's stomach clench. She had a strong feeling that what he referred to as conversation would be more like an interrogation.

Probably an "enhanced" interrogation. Laney tried to put a lid on the panic that rose inside her.

Considering he chose just to disguise his face, which consumed less magic than a complete transformation, he was probably conserving his energy for their "conversation."

Her own magic was strong but limited to earth materials. Everything in this office was synthetic. She frantically looked around, trying to spot something made of metal or stone. Technically, she could manipulate glass, since it originated from the natural materials of sand, soda ash, and sandstone. Still, as a human-made compound, it required more energy to bend to her will than she'd ever been able to harness.

Besides, against dark magic, she was pretty much helpless.

But she refused to give up.

Maybe if she kept him talking, some sort of solution would present itself. *Yeah, right*, the sarcastic voice inside her head whispered, but she squelched it. "What do you want?" She took another step and bumped into the wall behind her. "And how did you cloak your magic from me when we met last time?"

The man didn't bother getting closer. "I don't share my trade secrets." He smiled again, with just as little warmth as previously. "And I want the medallion, of course. After all, we paid you a lot of money to retrieve it for us."

Laney wondered briefly who "we" referred to, but dismissed the thought and concentrated on how to get out of this impossible situation. "You hired me under pretenses, though." Internally, she debated on how wise it was to contradict him, but had to keep *this* conversation going. That way, she didn't have to think about the future ones that the man had promised.

"I gave you all the paperwork that you requested." He tilted his head. "And you seemed very satisfied with them."

It was true. The paperwork that "Mr. Hartford" had presented, all checked out. He'd given Laney an authentication certificate and several documents that proved ownership. Obviously, they'd all been fakes. Excellent fakes because she had double and triple-checked their authenticity like she always did, and those documents were on record at various government agencies.

"But you knew they were fake," Laney insisted, her voice squeaking a little at the end of the sentence. She cleared her throat. "So, you violated the ethics clause I put in my contract."

The man threw his head back and laughed loudly. The shifting of his facial features sped up, and Laney had to swallow hard to keep from throwing up.

The faint sound of sirens wafted up from the street far below. A tiny flicker of hope rose in Laney's chest, even though she knew the first responders probably had nothing to do with her.

The man's laughter ended as abruptly as it had begun. "Enough," he said, throwing out his arm.

A bolt of magic hit Laney square in the chest. She struggled to inhale, and then everything went dark.

CHAPTER 4

Arek looked around the unassuming apartment in the Bernal Heights neighborhood of San Francisco. Either Dr. Elaine Marconi's housekeeping skills were sorely lacking, or someone had ransacked her home.

He'd bet on the latter.

He stood by two pieces of furniture that looked like they might make a dining room table if he glued them together. It would take a lot of glue. What he assumed had been matching chairs now looked mostly fit for kindling.

Considering that the building had a doorman and outside security cameras, this didn't seem a likely place for a random robbery. Plus, whoever broke in had taken the time to pick the lock and close the door after themselves. The intruders demolished the interior, but then closed the door so nobody would. They'd bought themselves some time.

But for what?

Did they not want Dr. Marconi's disappearance to be discovered?

Or had she not been there, and they were waiting for her to come back? Arek and Bolt had checked the surrounding area before they entered and had not noticed anyone lying in wait.

The entire apartment, except for the bedroom, had an open plan layout. You could stand anywhere and see everything else. Arek walked into the kitchen area, where the marble counter lay crushed into several pieces. Whoever had broken it had beyond-human strength. Based on the deep gashes marring the stone, he'd bet on shifters.

They'd opened every cupboard and shoved out the contents. Arek tried to avoid stepping on the mess of broken dishes, glasses, and spilled food on the floor, but it was impossible. Finally, he gave up and crunched his way out of the kitchen and over to where a shredded couch sat in front of a shattered, big flat screen TV.

Bolt gazed at the crooked empty rack on the wall. Just below it, a mess of wires poked out of a hole. "That's a Q900R screen," he said. Sadness tinted his voice. "It's top of the line and retails for almost forty K." He flicked a wire. "I get opening all the cabinets. But what did they think she was hiding inside her TV?" He looked down at the cracked screen.

Arek nodded. "I assume they wanted the medallion, but this is more than just searching. This is someone taking out their rage. She must have pissed them off."

"Maybe she held out for more money before she gave them the necklace." Bolt sniffed the air. "More than one person did this. And they reek of magic."

Arek drew in a deep breath. Bolt was right. The stink of magic lingered in the air, but it was worse than that. "Not just any magic. Dark magic." He rubbed the back of his head. "The grooves in the marble in the kitchen made me think shifters did this."

"Fuck," Bolt breathed out, looking around as if someone would jump out at them. He sniffed again. "Yeah. Shifters were here. I can't tell if they brought the magic or if it was already here."

Shifters and magic did not mix well. "Did you find anything about this woman performing blood sacrifices?"

His lieutenant shook his head. "No. I had to dig pretty deep into her file to find out why she'd left the university. If she is a dark witch, I'd have seen it in that search." Bolt had spent most of the morning running facial recognition software on various databases until he'd found their medallion thief in a university employment record.

After that, it was easy to figure out where she lived. Dr. Elaine Marconi once had been a revered expert on magical artifacts, but fell from grace when she slept with one of her students. Now she made her living as a thief for hire. Distaste curled Arek's lips into a snarl.

He looked around the apartment again. The place wasn't fancy, but not cheap either. San Francisco rents ran higher than average since water surrounded the city on three sides. There was no more land to build on unless you went south, down the peninsula. The interior of the place spoke, though, of an expensive taste. Even in shambles, the furniture and fixtures oozed good quality and taste.

He almost felt sorry for Dr. Marconi having to replace it all. Even the comfortable plush couch had become a target for the shifters' anger. White fluffs of stuffing spilled out of deep gashes in the cushions. "They smashed everything to pieces, but I don't see or smell any blood. Do you think she was here, and they took her?"

Bolt shook his head. "No. If she'd been here, it would have been quicker to make her tell them where the medallion was instead of searching for it. We'd probably see some blood from their interrogation." He flicked another torn wire sticking out of the wall. "Although if these shifters practice dark magic, maybe they used that."

"Banish that thought," Arek said. "These are not our wolves, and I don't want to contemplate the combination of rogue shifters and magic. It's bad enough that we're going to have to hunt these fuckers down as well as search for the medallion." *And Dr. Marconi,* he added as an afterthought.

He left Bolt to contemplate the sad fate of the TV and walked into the woman's bedroom. Shreds of fabric covered the floor. He couldn't tell if it was bedding or curtains.

The mattress leaned against a wall. Its springs were exposed. Fine fragments of wood that could at one point have been her box spring covered the floor.

A collapsed dresser lay beneath a hole in the wall. Bright-colored silky cloth spilled from the destroyed drawers. He hunched down and poked at one of them with a fingertip. Dr. Marconi's expensive taste in furniture extended to fine underwear.

Once again, he sniffed the air, trying to get a reading on who had destroyed the place, but the dark magic made it impossible to lock down on a scent trail. He knew these weren't his wolves, though. The pack bond would have told him.

Arek sniffed the air in the bedroom. Still no scent of blood.

He returned to Bolt, who had rigged up his laptop and rapidly typed on the keyboard while staring at the screen, a deep furrow on his brow.

Arek looked around again. "Why were these shifters so furious?" he wondered out loud. "They must not have found what they were looking for."

"I agree," Bolt said, turning the computer so that the screen faced Arek. "There were two wolves here, but they somehow cloaked themselves when they were in the elevator and hallway. The only security footage I could get is when they were in here and didn't bother hiding."

Arek glanced around the apartment, noticing small cameras in the corners of the room. "Fuck, I didn't think about us getting caught on video inside her apartment."

"I did," Bolt said. "I disabled the cameras everywhere in the building before we went in." They'd snuck up through the parking garage to bypass the doorman. Arek knew Bolt had disabled the cameras in the garage, but apparently, his lieutenant had thought further than that.

He leaned in to see what Bolt had uncovered by hacking into the surveillance system. Two men searched through the apartment. At first, they went methodically from room to room, opening and closing drawers and cabinets. The only thing giving them away as not human was their constant scenting of the air. Arek guessed he and Bolt would look like that on the footage, too, if it weren't for the forethought of his lieutenant.

Dr. Marconi seemed to have used her dining room table as a home office. She'd pushed it up against the wall and placed a lone chair beside it. In a corner, she'd stacked the rest. A laptop and piles of papers covered the table. On the screen, in the undestroyed living space, one wolf shifted partially. His hands sprung enormous claws that he used to shred the documents and destroy the laptop.

"Stupid," Bolt muttered. "There could be useful information on that computer."

"Do you know who they are?" Arek asked. His lieutenant had a photographic memory of faces and pelt patterns. The wolves on the screen grew impatient. Instead of methodically searching through shelves and drawers, they shoved everything out and flung it around.

"Nope. They're not part of a western pack. Unless someone has new recruits that we don't know about."

"They should have reported new pack members," Arek said slowly. Did he have a mutiny on his hands? Could an alpha that reported to him be so bold as to send new wolves into Arek's territory without asking permission?

The Pack Directives drawn up when the regional coalitions formed stipulated that any wolf outside of a pack must ask a region's Commanding Alpha for permission before entering a territory. These rogue wolves had not.

Pissed off, Arek continued watching the wolves on the screen as they continued their destruction of the apartment. Both of them had claws out now and the slashed and crushed indiscriminately. Bolt winced when they smashed the TV, and if it weren't for the dire thoughts of betrayal on Arek's mind, he would have chuckled.

Bolt turned the laptop back so that it faced him. "Nothing exciting happens. They just keep getting angrier." He tapped on the computer. "I'm sending a screenshot to Justice to see if he knows them. And I'll widen the search for matching footage outside the western region. If they're from another pack coalition and show up on a security camera in our territory, I'll find them."

"Start searching out east," Arek said, an awful feeling spreading through his body. "Nicholai Novikov, the Eastern Packs Coalition's alpha, started a conflict with the alphas of his neighboring packs to expand his territory eight months ago. And then he married a dark witch."

"That's where my thoughts went as well," Bolt said. "I'm already on it." He tapped the keyboard again. "And I'm checking traffic cameras to see where they went from here."

Arek paced the apartment while Bolt worked on the laptop.

A few months ago, Novikov had tried to kidnap the girlfriend of billionaire Magnus Flink, a lone wolf in Denver. He'd done so to force Flink to join the Eastern Packs so he would have to pay tithings to Novikov. Arek had been in Denver to warn Flink about Novikov's territory expansion and helped rescue Mina Parker, the girlfriend. She now worked remotely for Arek's security business by vetting his new clients. Magnus Flink still operated as a lone wolf, but as a consultant to the San Francisco Bay Area pack, he claimed ties with them.

After the Denver incident, Novikov had lain low, and Arek had hoped that would be the end. His gut feeling told him that the alpha and his dark witch were behind this, though.

His cell phone vibrated in his pocket simultaneously as Bolt's mobile beeped. Arek retrieved his device and checked the incoming message.

Justice's message displayed on the screen, "Novikov's wolves." Short and to the point.

"Fuck," Arek said.

Bolt hadn't bothered checking his phone. "It's as we suspected." He made it a statement and kept tapping the keyboard. "I have their car on camera. It's heading south."

Arek kept pacing, welcoming the rage that welled up inside him. Fucking Novikov.

Did he honestly think he could send wolves into Arek's territory and get away with it? Even worse, did he think he could send a disgraced witch to steal his medallion? "I want those wolves, and I want that woman," he growled.

"You'll get them," Bolt promised. After a few minutes, he stopped typing and looked up at Arek. "They're at a storage facility in San Mateo."

Arek strode to the door, his wolf so close to surface that he knew his eyes had turned ice-blue. "We know our pray now," he growled. "Time to start the hunt for real."

CHAPTER 5

Laney desperately needed water, but paradoxically, she also needed to pee. However, the pain in her arms distracted her from both the pressure in her bladder and her dry throat.

She'd regained consciousness a few hours ago, her wrists were tied together and looped over a hook that fastened in the ceiling. The man dressed in black had sat in a chair in front of her and laughed out loud when she awoke with a start and then scrambled to find her footage on the floor. The bastard had hung her just high enough to where her toes nudged the ground, but not enough to get traction so she could relieve her arms from taking the brunt of her weight.

Like a slab of slaughter on a meat hook.

After he'd had enough amusement, the man had started their "conversation."

As she had suspected earlier, Laney had not enjoyed it.

Her throat still ached from screaming, and if it weren't for the pain in her arms, she'd probably whimper from the lacerations covering her back. The man used both magic and an actual whip to shred her shirt and skin. A lone standing lamp by the opposite wall provided just enough light for her to see that the multi-tail flail leather tool now lay in a corner.

She wasn't sure how long the conversation had lasted because she'd passed out for a while. This did not please the man in black and he'd thrown water on her. She assumed it was water. It could have been magic for all she knew.

It had been cold. That's all Laney knew. Considering how hot the temperature inside the room was right now, she almost wished for another cold dousing.

She thought the man had left a few hours ago. Keeping track of time proved difficult between the waves of pain that shuddered through her body. She'd heard someone knock on what looked like a wall, but had turned out to be a shutter door.

The man had pulled it open, and then stepped outside. There'd been much shouting, and then the visitor and the man both left. She remembered hearing two sets of footsteps. At first, she'd been relieved, but now she wondered if they'd left her here to die.

It seemed a sad ending to her life, hanging from a hook in the ceiling, slowly twisting in a circle. Her view alternated between a very sad lamp, a cheap folding chair, and a multi-tailed whip. Although she hated it, someone finding her with the leather tool wasn't too bad. In the right circumstances, her suspended position and the flogging instrument could lead people to conclude she'd been on an adventurous date. However, the location—probably some kind of storage unit—and the sad lamp and cheap chair, were more signs of how far she'd fallen from her former glamorous life.

She giggled. The blood loss must have made her delirious if the thought of dying didn't bother her as much as people thinking she'd done so while on a cheap date. She couldn't help it. Laney would be much happier if her former colleagues, especially James, learned that she died while hanging from a fancy sex rack in luxurious accommodations instead of this sorry setup.

Of course, the lacerations on her back would probably have given away the torture. But maybe she'd developed a liking for rough sex. They could never know for sure. She laughed again, but it turned into a pitiful whimper.

Pulling herself together, Laney tried to raise herself higher again. Maybe if she just lifted her body a little, she could kind of jump and slip off the hook. But it was no use.

She didn't have enough strength left.

Should have done more crunches at the gym, lazy girl.

She chuckled, but that turned into a dry cough and just made her thirstier.

Screaming had made no one come to her aid during the "conversation," so she had no high hopes of attracting a rescuer if she yelled "help" now. Besides, her broken voice wouldn't carry very far.

She sniffed a little as a tear trailed down her cheek, but then defiantly blinked to dry her eyes. Wasting moisture was a bad idea when she was already so dehydrated.

A slight scratching sound from outside made Laney hold her breath to hear better. It sounded like claws scraping against metal.

Please, please, don't be rats.

She whimpered and then forced herself to be quiet. Compared to being eaten alive by rats, dying of dehydration and starvation—in a cheap BDSM setup—now seemed an infinitely more desirable way in which to leave this world.

Suddenly, the door flew open with a loud bang.

Laney blinked against the bright light piercing her eyes. It took her a little while to clear her vision, and when she did, she kept blinking because what she saw made little sense.

It had become night during the hours she'd been swinging on the hook. An intense light from the building opposite illuminated rain-spattered asphalt. Against that backdrop, stood two wolves that were the size of small ponies. One, slate gray with a white blaze running from the tip of its nose to its forehead, watched her with cold ice-blue eyes. The other's pelt glimmered silver in the light. Its forest green gaze was as chilly as the gray's.

Maybe she'd already died. But the breeze wafting in from the outside cooled her feverish skin, and that didn't seem like a detail she'd notice if she were unalive.

The gray wolf stepped into the room.

Laney shook her head wildly. "No," she tried to scream, but it came out a hoarse whisper from her cracked lips. She'd rather be eaten by rats than torn apart by wild beasts.

The air around the wolf shimmered, and Arek Varg stood in its place. A very naked, very muscular Arek Varg.

Laney blinked again. Yup. Probably already dead, despite her skin loving the cooler temperatures. Or at least close to the end of her life. Surely, fever dreams were a sign of being close to expiring?

"Dr. Marconi, I presume?" Varg asked.

Laney nodded, still staring, trying not to look lower than his face. She was in a lot of pain. But this was a splendid dream, and she couldn't help wondering what her subconscious would create below Varg's waist. Her gaze flicked down.

Yup. Ginormous. Her imagination had done well.

But just like that, the dream became a nightmare as he strode toward her, lifting his hands.

Laney couldn't help it. She flinched and whimpered, anticipating a blow.

Varg's eyes flashed, and he cursed under his breath. Moving slower, he turned her so that her side was to him. He supported her butt with one arm and hoisted her up. With the other, he lifted her off the hook.

As soon as Laney's feet touched the ground, she crumbled into a pile. She tried to hold inside a cry of pain, but a small whimper escaped. Everything hurt.

Another curse left Varg's lips, this one a little louder. "Run and get the car," he told the other wolf.

It growled in response and took off.

Laney pushed against the floor with her bound hands, but barely lifted her head.

Varg slowly crouched down next to her, extending his hand.

She swallowed hard but managed not to flinch this time.

"I've got you," he said and cupped her elbow.

With his help, Laney got up on her knees. That was as much energy as she had right now. She licked her lips. "What are you doing here?" His grip on her elbow felt very real. Even more real than her dry cracked lips

This was probably not a fever dream. Although sizzling sparks traveled up her arm from where he held her, so maybe it was. She shook her head to clear her mind, but all it did was make her head hurt.

"I believe you have something that belongs to me." His now azure eyes flickered to a much lighter color and then back again. He tilted his head and studied her, a very wolf-like gesture.

She licked her lips. "About that." Laney didn't know how to continue. What could she say? "Someone set me up," she finally settled on.

"I very much doubt that," Varg said.

She bristled. "What do you think happened here? Do you think I whip myself and then twirl around on meat hooks just for fun?" Somehow, her previous thoughts about adventurous sex combined with Varg's presence made her skin heat even more. A blush lit up her face, but she hoped he'd take it as a sign of anger.

He looked away for a beat, glancing up at the hook. "Maybe you were trying to take Novikov for more money, and he didn't like it."

"Who?" Laney asked.

"You're good." Varg smiled, but it wasn't a cheerful expression. "But you're not fooling me twice."

The sound of screeching tires came from down the row of storage units, and Varg quickly moved so that she was behind him. His shoulders tensed and his fists clenched.

When an unobtrusive black sedan came into view, he relaxed and turned to face Laney. "Can you stand?"

She managed to get vertical with his help, but her legs wouldn't hold her when he let go. Varg scooped her up and carried her over to the car.

She considered protesting, but what was the point? Her body's weakness made it impossible to walk, or even stand, on her own. She hated being helpless, even if it involved a sexy, muscular, and very naked man carrying her.

Man? Or wolf? What was the correct term for a shifter? The thoughts threatened to short-circuit her brain, so she left them alone. For now.

The driver's side door opened, and a man dressed in gray sweats and a hoodie covering his head got out. Dark stubble graced his chiseled chin. He watched her with the same intensely green eyes as those of the silver wolf. His gaze was just as hostile as the beast's had been.

"Get the blanket from the trunk," Varg told him.

The other man sighed but did as asked and wrapped it around Laney. He then opened the rear door of the car.

Suddenly shivering, she huddled into the warm piece of fabric as Varg gently positioned her in the back seat. He stepped around the car. When he came back into view, he too wore sweats, but with a t-shirt. If the pain hadn't distracted her, Laney would have mourned the disappearance of his fine body.

She held out her hands. "Can you cut me loose, please?"

Varg laughed. "Not a chance, witch." He closed the door in her face and got in the driver's seat.

The other man entered from the front passenger door.

Varg watched her through the rearview mirror. His eye color had returned to ice-blue. "You have until we get home to tell me where you hid the medallion."

Laney sighed. "What do you think I'm going to do if you release my hands? Zap you and run away? I don't even have enough energy to make my legs work. If I could throw energy bolts, don't you think I would have sizzled off the restraints by now?"

"I'm not taking any chances." Varg ignited the engine and drove the car forward.

The other man spoke for the first time, "Good thinking. Witches are tricky."

Laney sighed again, but inwardly this time. She'd not met a shifter before, but she'd heard they despised all forms of magic. "There's nothing tricky about my powers," she said. "It's just another ability. Like shifting into a wolf, for example. You'd think even wolves would be more evolved than holding on to old prejudices by now."

The two men in the front exchanged a look that spoke volumes about their opinions on comparing magic to shifting. They obviously disagreed.

Laney tried to pull the blanket more tightly around her, but it was hard with her bound hands. She met Varg's gaze in the mirror and held up her hands again.

He shook his head. "Start talking," he said.

So much for chivalry.

Laney took a deep breath. "I retrieve stolen artifacts for insurance companies," she began.

The man in the passenger seat twisted his body and faced her. "You mean you're a thief," he said in an icy voice. "Don't dress it up."

She sighed inwardly. This was going to be a long car ride.

At least she had the medallion as a bargaining chip. Hopefully, negotiations with Varg would not involve torture.

CHAPTER 6

Arek studied his reluctant house guest from across the dinner table. Their arrival at the Pack House had her pissed off, and she was still fuming. Somehow, she'd thought he meant her apartment when he said he'd take her home. Her amber-golden eyes glittered dangerously as they met his. She wore sweats. He had piles of them on hand for whenever pack members needed a change of clothes after shifting. The ones she'd chosen were a little too big. The top had slipped down her shoulder, revealing honey-colored skin he'd love to taste if they'd met under different circumstances. And if she hadn't been in so much pain.

Because of her injuries, Dr. Marconi sat very straight in her chair. Their pack doctor had examined her wounds and determined that, although the lacerations were severe, they didn't need stitches. As long as they could keep them from being infected, Dr. Marconi should be okay. Arek's jaw clenched.

That asshole Novikov had whipped her back to shreds. Sadistic bastard.

He'd suggested his guest take her meal in her room, but she'd refused and insisted on joining him for dinner. One thing he'd learned about Dr. Marconi so far, she was stubborn as hell. Despite being tortured by Novikov, she kept the medallion's whereabouts quiet.

Arek would, of course, never physically hurt her for the information, but she didn't know that.

"Is the food not to your liking?" he asked as he chewed his excellent steak.

She lowered those striking amber-colored eyes to stare at the utensils in front of her. He missed her gaze, even if it had shot daggers at him. She picked up her fork and knife and cut a piece of the meat. "It's great," she said. "My compliments to the chef. I guess I'm just not hungry."

"I'll let her know you enjoyed the meal, but you need to eat more," Arek said. "You've lost much blood and need to replenish with both nutrition and liquids." He pointedly took a sip of his water glass.

She sighed but drank some water and then kept eating. "I still don't understand why I couldn't just go home. You know where I live now, so it's not like you couldn't keep tabs on me." She quirked an eyebrow. "Especially since you've hacked into my surveillance system." Bolt had shown her the footage of her destroyed apartment, but instead of being outraged over the damage, Dr. Marconi expressed anger over the fact that they could "spy" on her "like perverts."

Arek smiled at the memory. Mid-sentence of Dr. Marconi's tirade, his lieutenant had calmly stood and walked out. She'd sputtered insults after Bolt. Some of them were very creative. "Why are you so set on returning when it's not safe? Until we catch the shifters that destroyed your place and neutralize Novikov, you are in danger, Dr. Marconi."

"Laney," She tilted her head and winced when the gestured must have pulled the skin on her back. Red highlights glimmered as her wavy brown hair moved. "I asked you to call me Laney."

"There's also the small matter of returning my medallion, Laney." He emphasized her name but would keep thinking of her as Dr. Marconi. It was safer that way. The little witch already tempted and distracted him. With Novikov and his wolves running wild in Arek's territory, he could afford neither.

A faint blush spread across her cheeks. "Yes, yes. The medallion," she muttered. "I've already apologized profusely about that. I told you, the man you think is Novikov set up a whole fake insurance company and gave me counterfeit paperwork."

Arek didn't quite believe that story, but something had obviously gone sour between her and Novikov. Whatever the reason, he couldn't just send her out there on her own. Justice and Bolt were looking for the Eastern Packs'

Commanding Alpha and his shifters. "I don't care why you stole it," he said. "I just want to know where my talisman is, and when I will have it back."

She put down her cutlery and deliberately took her time chewing and swallowing. That amber gaze met his again. After he'd dealt with Novikov—and she'd return the Odin medallion—he'd like to seduce her just to see what those gorgeous eyes looked like when filled with passion. "Look," she said. "I have one bargain chip here, and it's that damn necklace. I'd be stupid to just give it up without some kind of guarantee that I'll make it out of this situation alive."

Gorgeous and smart. "And why would I trust a bargain with a thief?" He chuckled. "And why would I honor an agreement with someone who stole from me?" She looked away and swallowed hard. Dr. Marconi wasn't as unafraid as she pretended to be. Good. She should be wary of him. Because of more reasons than him physically hurting her.

He wanted to lick all that honey skin from top to toe. He wanted to devour her. And he would, once he'd taken care of Novikov. Dr. Marconi should definitely be on her guard.

She fiddled with the fork on the side of her plate. "You have a reputation for being a fair man."

"Tell me where the medallion is, and I will treat you fairly."

A wry smile played on her lips. "I think I'll hold on to my bargaining chip a little longer. But I'll tell you something that will make you feel better. It's in a safe place."

That did not fucking make him feel better.

With Novikov running loose in his territory, he needed the amulet back around his neck. But he'd play her game a little longer because he didn't relish having to scare the woman into believing he'd hurt her.

Besides, he had wolves searching her place again, now that the stench of dark magic should have faded. If the medallion was there, they'd find it. "Then we're at an impasse because you'll stay here until I get my medallion back."

She scoffed. "What do you expect me to do while I'm here? Just rattle around in this huge mansion, bored out of my mind?" She gestured wildly, and he assumed the movement meant the entire house. It wasn't a mansion, but pack members sometimes stayed with him for a while, so he needed a lot of extra bedrooms. Like the one Dr. Marconi was currently occupying.

Plus, Justin and Bolt had their quarters here. And his chef had insisted on a professional kitchen, both in terms of equipment and size. And they needed a gym, which had required an addition since the room that housed his collection of magical artifacts took up the entire basement.

Okay, so it was a big house, but not a *mansion*.

"That's not my concern," he countered, but an idea that had brewed in his mind since they'd first gotten back to the house solidified. "Although there might be something you can help me with."

She eyed him warily. "What?"

"Finish your meal, and I'll tell you."

She sighed again but picked up her fork and continued eating.

Arek unlocked the door to the room in the basement that the wolves called "the vault." They'd named it that because lead shielding covered each wall and the door.

Dr. Marconi fidgeted beside him. "Are you going to show me your dungeon?" Underneath her brave words, her voice shook with nervousness.

Inwardly, he smiled but kept any sign of that off his face. Instead, he leaned toward her, close enough that she could feel his breath on her skin. "Do you want me to show you my dungeon?" She smelled delicious. Like peaches and cream. The temptation to lick and nip her gorgeous honey-golden skin grew stronger.

No doubt about it. She would end up in his bed.

And when she did, he would devour her.

A deep flush crept up her neck and cheeks. "No," she sputtered.

Arek chuckled. He'd known she'd turn him down. He wouldn't have flirted with her if that hadn't been a guaranteed outcome. "This is where I keep my collection." He gestured for her to proceed ahead of him. "Depending on how you play your cards, I'll show you my dungeon later."

"I don't want to see your dungeon. I mean, I don't believe you have a—oh, wow." She stepped into the room and slowly turned in a circle. "This is amazing."

He looked around the space, trying to see it with her eyes. To an expert in magical artifacts, it would probably appear a treasure trove. To him, it was just storage for items that could hurt his wolves. Since he'd been alive for more than a century, the collection included quite a few items.

Dr. Marconi trailed her fingers along the shelves as she perused the items encased in various boxes and chests. Some of them were as old as the items they contained. Some of them had attached placards with the object's name, but for many of the items, he had no idea what they were. If they contained magic, someone could use them to hurt a shifter, so he'd acquire it and dump it in here.

"How have you kept this a secret?" Dr. Marconi whispered. "You're supposed to report relics with power to a university's magical artifacts department."

Arek frowned. Maybe it had been a mistake showing her this. "Says who?"

She turned to face him. "Says the Witch and Mage Council."

He dismissed her words with a hand gesture. "I'm not a witch or a mage. I don't answer to them."

She opened her mouth, but then closed it again. "I suppose not," she finally said with a bit of a chuckle. Her eyes glittered. "Oh, man, they'd be so pissed if they'd find out about the treasures you keep here."

"Who would tell them?" An edge crept into his voice.

Dr. Marconi did that head-tilt-and-wince gesture again. "Well, I sure won't. I owe no loyalty to them. Quite the opposite." She stepped up to one shelf where none of the items had descriptions. "Is that an Arminian gold sacrificial dagger?" Leaning closer, a sigh escaped her lips. "Goddess bless me. That must be a thousand years old." She clenched her fists as if to keep from touching the item. "It's exquisite."

Arek shrugged. "Don't know. Don't care. I only want it out of the way so it can't hurt my wolves."

She turned toward him again. "Why are you showing me all of this?"

"You said you wanted to have something to do while you were here. You could catalog these for me. And make sure they're properly stored."

"You have all these treasures, but you haven't kept a record?" Incredulity laced her voice.

He looked around the room. "There are some ledgers around somewhere where I jotted things down. It'd be more practical to create a proper database."

Dr. Marconi stared at him, her mouth opening and closing. "You're serious," she finally choked out. "You just dumped all these things in here?" She swept out her arm. "And you have no clue where they came from, how old they are, or what they can do?"

"It hasn't been a priority to keep track," Arek said, feeling vaguely guilty and pissed off that she could make him feel that way. "I've been busy with other stuff. If the item came with information, I wrote that down." He looked around the room again. Where the fuck were those notebooks?

"But you'll let me work with these artifacts? I get to examine them?" Her eyes widened. "All of them?"

He nodded. "If you want to." Until he got the medallion back, he'd know where she was.

Right now, he chose not to examine why that pleased him immensely.

She stepped deeper into the room, walking along the shelves at a clip. "Okay, I need a laptop, a crapload of salt, and a big tank of water."

Arek grinned. So much for being bored while staying at the Pack House. He'd found the perfect way to distract the little witch while he hunted down the medallion and dealt with Novikov.

After that, he looked forward to getting to know Dr. Marconi better. Especially in bed.

He had some time before that could happen. Her wounds had to heal first.

Fucking Novikov. He'd pay for what he'd done to her lovely skin.

CHAPTER 7

Laney had just finished her shower when someone knocked on the door to the enormous suite where she'd spent the night. She circumvented a jetted tub big enough for four people and reached for the fluffy bathrobe hanging on the back of the door. She knew Varg was wealthy, but the scale of his fortune had not hit home until she'd seen this part of his house. Granite tiles covered the bathroom floors and walls. She'd slept through the night in a king-sized bed, resting on sheets with a tread count several digits higher than she could afford for herself.

She really wanted to get back into the room with all the artifacts, but Bolt was supposed to give her a tour of the rest of the house this morning. If that was him on the other side of the door, he was early. And judging from another hard knock, impatient.

She pulled on the robe and winced as the soft terrycloth touched her abused back. "Just a minute," she called, frantically toweling her hair as she walked to get the door. She belted her robe more securely and opened the door to find, just as expected, Bolt on the other side.

They'd agreed to meet first thing in the morning, but she thought that meant that she would have time to take a shower and eat breakfast first. "You're too early," she said in the way of greeting.

"It was supposed to be first thing," Bolt answered, stepping into the suite without being asked. He carried a tray with him and walked straight into the adjacent sitting room to deposit it on the polished marble-topped side table. "I brought breakfast," he said, gesturing to the tray.

He grabbed one plate covered with a silver dome and sat down at the small dining table. It was just as polished and made of just as heavy wood as the rest of the furnishings in the suite.

"Good morning to you too," Laney said and lifted the cover on the remaining plate. Eggs Benedict with baby spinach and a mountain of fresh fruit greeted her. She took a deep breath, appreciating the tantalizing aroma of the food. "This smells heavenly."

Bolt made a sound somewhere between a snort and a laugh.

"What?" Laney grabbed a rolled-up cloth napkin with silverware and carried her plate to the table.

"It just always amazes me how humans can't smell anything until they already see what it is." Bolt shoveled eggs and hollandaise sauce into his mouth like someone would pull his plate away at any minute. His plate had four muffins and eggs, compared to her two. Instead of fresh fruit, a tall pile of hash browns rose from the plate, threatening to topple and bury the other food. Apparently, there were non-shifter portions and shifter portions in this house.

"No potatoes for me?" Laney asked. The hash browns would taste good with the hollandaise sauce.

He stopped a loaded fork in midair and gave her a surprised look. "Did you want some?" He lifted his dish, ready to shovel some of his hash browns onto her plate.

"I'll trade you some fruit," she said.

He looked at her plate for a moment. "Nah," he said finally, shoveling a third of his potatoes on her plate. "I'm good. I don't eat that stuff."

"That stuff?" Laney asked. "Fruit and vegetables?"

Bolt nodded. "Not enough calories per volume for a shifter. Especially after a shift."

"You just shifted?"

He paused for a beat and looked away. "Well, I went for a morning run."

How freaking early did shifters rise? Laney looked out the floor-to-ceiling windows. Next to them, French doors led to a balcony. She'd noticed the spectacular view of Bonita Cove from the bedroom window when she first got up.

The night before, it had been too dark to figure out the house's location. Now, though, she could tell they were obviously in the Marin Headlands somewhere. Across the Golden Gate Bridge from San Francisco. "I've hiked this area several times and never noticed buildings. I thought the state owned and protected this land. How did Varg get building permits?"

Bolt gestured vaguely with his fork. "This building has been here since before the state bought up the land. It's been pack land forever. The first alpha who built a cabin on this site negotiated with the people who have true claim to the land, the Coastal Miwok."

Laney sat back. "The wolves have been here since before the English and Spanish arrived?" That was a long freaking time.

"The wolves lived in harmony with the original people and helped to fight the English and the Spanish. Many of the wolves had Miwok true mates." Bolt kept eating.

"True mates?"

He put down his fork. "A wolf's true love, their mate for life. You don't know very much about shifters, do you?"

Laney shook her head. "I used to work at the university's magical artifacts department and curated their museum—"

"I know that story already," Bolt interrupted.

Laney stopped. Of course, he knew. They must have researched her to find her address. Which meant the wolves knew about her disgraced departure as well. She took a deep breath and continued, ignoring the interruption. "And my colleagues and I knew about shifters, of course. But since you don't socialize with mages and witches, it's hard to document information about you." You could only learn so much from secondary sources like manuscripts and online resources. The most accurate learning came from first-hand sources.

Bolt nodded. "We don't want to be documented. Especially not by people who wield magic."

"How does that make sense? Why the prejudice against my kind?" She knew shifters were averse to magic, but the ability to shift was just another side of magic.

"In my case, I have a good reason," Bolt muttered and shoveled in the last of his food.

"What about pack magic? Why is that allowed but not other kinds?"

"Pack magic would not hurt a shifter unless they deserved it."

Laney waited, but apparently, that was all the wolf would share. She changed the topic. "Did you grow up in this pack?" Learning more about Varg and his pack would be helpful to her negotiations.

"No," Bolt said, scraping his plate and looking at what remained on hers. "Are you done with breakfast?"

She pushed the plate over to him. He pushed the fruit to the side and dug in. "Where are you from then?"

"I have no idea." When Laney made a surprised sound, Bolt looked up from his plate. "Arek found Justice and me in the fighting pits. I have no memory of my life before that."

She swallowed a gasp. The brutal world of underground prizefighting had a dark reputation of indentured combatants that had to fight to earn their freedom. "What's your earliest memory, then?"

He studied her for a beat. "I was about twelve, and someone, maybe a parent, told me I had to listen to the fight master from now on."

She couldn't keep her gasp from escaping. "Your parents sold you to the fighting pits?"

Bolt shrugged. "It happens to many shifter kids sometimes because their parents need money. Sometimes because they don't know how to handle a kid who turns into a predatory animal at inopportune times." She opened her mouth to ask more, but he stood and gathered their dishes. "That's enough chitchat. Let's get going." He dumped their plates back on the tray. His loud clattering of dishes made it clear there'd be no more discussing the past.

He walked toward the door of the suite.

Laney cleared her throat. "Um, I need to get dressed first."

He turned around and looked at her as if he'd not even noticed her wet hair, robe, or dripping towel draped over her shoulders. "Oh. How long will that take?"

She sighed and walked through to the bedroom and en suite bathroom. "As long as it takes," she said over her shoulder and closed the door between them.

Laney quickly straightened the sheets on the bed and pulled up the bed cover before piling the pillows she'd thrown on the floor the night before on top of the bedding. The mattress had been soft enough to cradle her sore body but firm enough to relax her cramped back.

She'd always appreciated quality stuff, but the furnishings that Arek Varg had in his house were leagues above what she had treated herself with when she outfitted her apartment in Bernal Heights.

The thought of her nice table, chairs, couch, and bed smashed to pieces made her sigh. Her savings would deplete significantly when she replaced all of that. And not just furniture, but dishes, clothes, and bedding. She'd have to start from scratch. Arek said most of her clothes were okay. He'd had a funny grin on his face when he told her, but wouldn't explain why.

She went into the bathroom to brush the snarls out of her hair. She'd found toiletries in the granite-covered vanity, all brand new. A cabinet contained a brush, a hairdryer, even some styling products. Opening a drawer even revealed fancy-branded unopened makeup. Either Arek Varg didn't want company in his bed after he'd seduced someone, or he had a lot of overnight visitors staying with him. Maybe a combination of both. Her cheeks heated when she thought of Varg in bed.

To distract herself, Laney opened a fresh toothbrush, squeezed some paste out from a travel-size tube, and began cleaning her teeth.

The idea of starting over new didn't hurt as much emotionally as it did financially. She'd bought all her stuff when she first started at the university. Back then, as a revered academic with a busy social life, she'd often entertained in her apartment. Not so much since her fall from grace.

Maybe she should think about getting a smaller place. A studio would probably be enough space for her now. Besides, rents in San Francisco were sky-high. It would be a good idea to cut back on that expense. Especially now that it didn't look like she would get paid for retrieving the medallion.

She spat and rinsed.

The reflection looking back at her in the mirror didn't look too bad, considering she'd spent most of yesterday hanging from a meat hook. Her arms were still sore and her back hurt like hell. Bruising colored underneath her eyes, but other than that, she looked okay from her ordeal.

As she peeled off the bathrobe, her wounds protested, though. She turned so she could see her back in the mirror. Whatever stuff the pack's doctor had slathered on her gashes had helped. They were still red, but none bled, and they looked clean and healthy. Being an earth-bound witch also gave her the advantage of accelerated healing.

She padded naked into the bedroom and opened the big armoire that matched the bed's dark wood. Inside were piles of sweats, yoga pants, and t-shirts in various colors and sizes, as well as cotton panties and sports bras. She chose a deep blue t-shirt that made her think of Varg's eyes and a pair of light gray yoga pants. On her feet, she put on fresh crew socks and then laced up the brand new black and blue trainers she'd the night before found in her size.

She returned to the bathroom and dug out a hair fastener to put her still-wet hair in a ponytail. That would have to do.

Bolt's first words to her when she stepped out of the bedroom were, "About time."

Laney smiled. He'd waited only ten minutes. "You don't have a partner, do you?"

He gave her a startled look. "What does that have to do with anything?"

She chuckled. "Nothing."

"Why do you want to know?" He eyed her suspiciously. "Are you flirting with me? I'm not interested in witches."

Laney burst out laughing. "I'm not hitting on you, but that's good to know."

"Look, do you want this tour or not?" Bolt sounded irritated and started walking down the hall.

"Yes," Laney answered, following in his footsteps. The faster she learned the house's layout, the quicker she could figure out how to get the hell out of here. Although, that meant leaving Varg's treasure trove behind.

Her former boss and colleagues would burst from envy if they knew about Varg's collection.

She stopped. If she told them about what she had seen, would they give her back her old job? For so long, she'd wanted nothing else but to get back her reputation and her career. But now that maybe she had the means to do so, the thought wasn't as tempting. They'd scorned her and planted false rumors.

Ruined her reputation so well that no other university would hire her.

"What's the holdup?" Bolt shot from further down the hallway. He'd only now noticed she'd stopped.

Laney thought about the many priceless artifacts a few floors below them. The perfect revenge against her former colleagues would be if she published about Varg's collection in academic journals on her own. She'd name him as “an eccentric collector who wished to remain anonymous” and never reveal his name. Picturing James’s face when he read her work sent a wave of pleasure through her body. “Nothing,” she said as she smiled and walked toward Bolt. “Nothing at all.”

The wolves had no idea what priceless artifacts they'd collected over the years. She couldn't wait to examine and study them all and retaliate against the university.

Something deep inside her stirred.

Something she'd suppressed for a long time.

For the first time in almost two years, she felt the familiar hunger that she’d thought lost forever. The passion she’d thought lost forever. The yearning that had once been her reason for existing.

The desire to search for clues about what had once been. How it had shaped ancient empires and cultures. How it still influenced society today.

She couldn't wait to get back down in that basement.

CHAPTER 8

Arek logged out of the video conference software and closed down his laptop. The discussion with the other alphas in the Western Packs Coalition had gone okay. As well as expected, considering the purpose of the call was to inform them that an intruder was in their territory.

The coalition met monthly, and Arek loathed the obligation because, although the wolves understood the necessity of being in a partnership, they were all alphas. Getting them to agree on anything could be exhausting. However, today's call had given them a common enemy. Nothing united a group of alphas as quickly as the possibility of a good fight. Well, as united as a bunch of domineering wolves could be.

Although everyone wanted to oust the interloper, they had not agreed on a plan that would accomplish that.

Some of them called for a public execution. Others wanted to know Novikov's motivation before they acted.

Arek just wanted the Russian and his wolves out of the Bay Area's pack territory.

He shouldn't complain about the alphas he governed, however. Compared to the politics of some of the other coalitions, the Western Pack's was relatively frictionless.

On one occasion, a younger wolf tried to instigate infighting within the alliance to advance his standing within the packs. The alpha of the pack to which the youngster belonged had snuffed out the rebellion before anything serious became of it.

For the most part, the Western Packs Coalition alphas saw the benefits of having a union. It discouraged fighting over territories and resources while giving access to a significant number of fighting wolves and weapons when facing an outside enemy.

Like now. When Arek's pack had to deal with Novikov.

Nora Bretagne, their legal advisor, entered the office. "I researched the travel records as you requested," she said. Except for Bolt, Nora was the best hacker in his pack. She combined those skills with a brilliant strategic mind, and Arek often thought of her as his secret weapon.

The macho wolf culture constantly underestimated Nora, and she knew how to use that to her advantage. "No Nicholai Novikov traveled to the western states in the last six months. I can go back further if you want me to."

Arek sighed. "No. He wouldn't have been able to stay hidden that long. Thank you, though." He'd asked Nora to check all modes of long-distance travel to California or neighboring states, just in case Novikov drove the last part of the journey to avoid detection. "The bastard is probably traveling under an assumed name. Can we check security film from airports, as well as train and bus stations, and run facial recognition?"

"Yes, but wait. I got more." Nora held up her hand, interrupting him. They'd known each other for a long time, and she treated him as a brother. Sometimes she became overly familiar, but rarely disrespectful. He didn't mind. Arek preferred people who called him on his shit, whether or not he wanted them to. "I also checked hotels and house rentals in Northern California to see if anyone by that name had checked in or rented a place." She smiled. "I'm not just a pretty face, you know."

Arek returned her grin. Nora's features were striking, and people often stopped to stare because her mere presence commanded attention. However, she thought their attention was because of a large scar that ran from the corner of her right brow, across her eye, and down to the top of her lip. It marked her as a warrior, but Nora used self-deprecating humor whenever she commented on her looks. She probably thought the scar marred her looks. "Your face is beautiful and strong," he said, "but your amazing brain is what I fell in love with."

She laughed. "Oh please, I'm not one of your conquests. Save the flattery and the killer smile for someone it will work on."

Arek grinned. "Fine, tell me what you found."

"No Novikovs are staying in the Bay Area or the immediately adjacent regions." Nora looked down at a tablet in her hand. "However, I found an Inessa Aslanova and Iakov Aslanov at a DoubleTree hotel in Modesto."

"Inessa is the name of Novikov's new wife," Arek said.

Nora smiled again. "I know. And after doing some digging, which took a while because she's erased a lot of personal data, but not even dark magic can eliminate all cyber tracks. I discovered Aslanova is her mother's last name."

"So, her maiden name?"

"No, her maiden name is her father's last name, and Inessa used the female version, Butosova, before she married Novikov. Her brother, however, has always used the male version of their mother's last name."

"Her brother?" Arek echoed. "And female and male last names?" His head hurt.

Nora nodded. "Russian last names have different endings depending on whether the person who bears them is male or female." She shook her head. "Very backwoods and binary specific, I know." She tapped a finger against the tablet. "But my point is, there are two siblings who wield dark magic in our territory, Inessa and Iakov."

"Oh, fuck."

"My sentiments exactly," Nora said. "Nicholai may not even be here. He sent his wife and brother-in-law instead."

Arek growled. "Doesn't matter. He's still trespassing uninvited on pack territory."

Nora looked away and cleared her throat. "About that. It's not as clear as you might think."

"What are you talking about?"

"Well, according to the Pack Directives that were drawn up when the coalitions formed, any wolf of an outside pack must ask permission from the Commanding Alpha before entering a territory and should also inform the local pack alpha of them being in the area. However, Nicholai could claim that since Inessa and Iakov are not wolves, the rules do not apply."

"That's bullshit." Arek banged his fist on the table. "Everyone knows it applies to all pack members of an outside pack. We discussed the law's intent when that rogue wolf and his human true mate infringed on the Central Packs' territory. The wolf argued the rules didn't apply to his mate since she wasn't a wolf, but the intent of the law determined the outcome of the case."

Nora nodded. "Yes, there was much discussion. But nobody updated the Pack Directives, so the original wording of the law remains 'wolf.' The Eastern Packs' lawyer was supposed to update the documents to say 'member' instead. But when he died in that accident, it never happened."

Arek sighed. "An accident orchestrated by Nick Novikov, no doubt."

"Very likely," Nora agreed. "The lawyer worked for the previous alpha that Novikov challenged and killed and refused to step down when the regime changed."

Fucking politics. Fucking Eastern Packs' ambitious alpha. "Is there a way to keep track of the dark witch and her brother?"

"I've reached out to some contacts in the Sacramento pack. They agreed to travel to Modesto. Hopefully, they'll find the siblings' vehicle and install a tracker." She shrugged. "I wouldn't get my hopes up, however. The two of them must know that you'll want to put surveillance on them once you discover they're here."

"What about the two wolves that we caught on camera in Dr. Marconi's apartment?"

Nora sighed. "I don't have any information on them other than that they are members of Novikov's pack. They seem to have vanished after they broke into Dr. Marconi's apartment." She hugged the tablet to her. "By the way, what are you going to do about her?"

"What do you mean?" Arek avoided Nora's direct gaze.

"You can't just imprison her and keep her under house arrest. The Witch and Mage Council will eventually find out and insist you either take legal action against her or let her go."

Spoken just like a lawyer, but Arek doubted the council would involve themselves much in Dr. Marconi's case. They seemed to have washed their hands of her when they made her resign from her university and museum posts. "She's not a prisoner. She can leave anytime she wants. All she has to do is give me the medallion."

Nora's eyebrows shot to the top of her forehead. "Have you told her she can leave without punishment as soon as you have the medallion?"

Of course, he hadn't told her that.

It would defeat the purpose of having her scared enough to give up the medallion. Although that had backfired. Doctor Marconi thought she had to hold on to the artifact for protection from him. "She knows," he lied to Nora.

"Mm-hm," she answered, one eyebrow quirked. He avoided her knowing look. Maybe it wasn't all that good to surround himself with people that called him out on his bullshit. Nora waved her hand. "Anyway, how about you show her a picture of Inessa and Iakov? It could have been either of them who held her captive in the storage facility. I'm sure Inessa can take on a male form." She handed him a printout. In the image, a man and a woman wearing fancy evening wear smiled at a camera. It looked like they were at some kind of society gala. Both of them were tall and icy blond. They looked remarkably alike.

"Are they twins?" Arek asked.

Nora shook her head. "No, Inessa is two years older. But, of course, one perk of being a dark witch, or mage, is that you don't age."

"Until the magic claims its prize." Arek countered. Every time a practitioner performed a dark magic spell or rite, they lost part of their humanity. Old folklore said they put a stain upon their soul. Eventually, no humanity remained, and the mage or witch either withered and died—soulless—or, in some rare cases, became a ravenous beast that hunted and devoured all other creatures, especially supernatural beings.

He shook himself out of those dark thoughts. "Let's go find Dr. Marconi and show her this picture. I want you to meet her and tell me what you think of her."

"I already like her," Nora said as she walked out of the office. "I heard her talking to Bolt when they passed my office during their house tour. She's driving him mad with all her questions."

Arek chuckled. One reason he'd asked Bolt to do the tour was because he knew the tight-lipped wolf wouldn't share information he shouldn't.

Also, the only other person he'd trust with Dr. Marconi, Justice, was currently searching her apartment again, looking for where she'd hidden the medallion.

And Justice was a big flirt, which was the other reason Arek didn't want him anywhere near Dr. Marconi.

CHAPTER 9

Laney fell in love with the spectacular sunroom on the second floor. A few feet of solid ceiling jutted out of the mansion corner where the room abutted the house. The rest of the roof, and the walls, were made entirely of glass. She could spend days just watching the view from here. To the west, Bonita Cove's beaches framed the half-circle bay that ended in the skinny Point Bonita peninsula and its lone lighthouse. Beyond that, the blue waters of the Pacific Ocean stretched until the horizon. A straight line from where she currently lay curled up on a day lounger—neglecting a few atolls—the next solid landfall would be Japan. This, of course, was true from any point in San Francisco, but the impact of all that water hit harder here when she saw it stretched out for miles and miles.

She twisted so she could look out to the east. Out of an enormous fog bank, the Golden Gate Bridge rose majestically. Its red color contrasted dramatically with the fog's gray and the dark blue of the swirling waters underneath. The landmark seemed to claim its place with such confidence that Laney couldn't even imagine what it would have been like for people to live in the area without the bridge. Before its completion in the 1930s, everything on the north side of the bridge, where she was now, would have been so isolated. But maybe that was how the wolves and the Coastal Miwok tribe had preferred it.

Laney adjusted her position again and looked straight ahead out the windows. She had to stretch her neck a little to see the end of Point Diablo, which caused a twinge in her back. But it was less painful than before, and she admired the small white shack with the blinking light that warned incoming ships of the protruding land hazard.

"Are you done yet?" Bolt wanted to know. He stood next to Laney's lounger despite the fact that there were several equally comfortable loungers and chairs on which he could rest his butt. Instead, he hovered over her, his arms crossed and a miserable frown on his face.

"Nope." She gestured toward the cozy furniture scattered around the room. "Why don't you rest for a while? Tell me some more about the pack and how it works?" Potted palms and other large plants thrived in the sunlit room. How could he not want to just relax for a bit in the beautiful space?

Bolt remained standing, and the furrows above his brows deepened. "I haven't told you anything about how the pack works."

"Exactly," Laney said. She must have asked a hundred questions during their house tour, and except for details about how the exercise equipment in the gym worked, Bolt had divulged nothing useful. "I'm supposed to work with Varg's artifacts, but I know nothing about pack customs or rules."

"None of the items in the basement come from the pack." Bolt rubbed his palm over the short stubble on top of his head.

"How do you know?"

"Because the pack doesn't do magic. We contain Arek's collection in the basement vault to keep anyone from using the artifacts against shifters."

Laney tilted her head so she could better watch Bolt's face without the sun in her eyes. "But the Odin medallion has power, and that's not kept in that room."

He stilled and narrowed his eyes. "No, it doesn't."

She felt like saying, "does too," in a sing-song voice, but decided that was a little too childish. "I felt it when I touched it."

Bolt took a menacing step forward and leaned over her, his face close to hers. "Whatever you think you felt. I would advise you to keep that detail to yourself."

A chill slid down Laney's spine, but not because Bolt scared her. He looked menacing, but she didn't think he'd hurt her without physical provocation. The cold sliver came from finally discovering something useful. Maybe this secret strengthened her position at the bargaining table. She sat up straighter and stared right back at the wolf. "And if I don't?"

"What's going on here?" Arek Varg asked from the doorway, hand on hips. The cream cable-knit sweater, perfectly molded to his chest, looked thin yet warm. Another piece of expensive clothing. He aimed his piercing blue eyes at Laney, but she couldn't interpret their expression.

Behind the alpha stood a tall woman with flaming red hair, styled in a chin-length bob. Her hand covered her mouth, and from the delight glittering in her eyes, Laney thought she attempted to hide a smile. A jagged white line on her skin ran from her brow to the top of her lip, but it detracted nothing from her gorgeous face.

Bolt straightened and took a step back. He looked at Laney and shook his head in annoyance. "Just don't," he said. He turned toward the door. "Boss, may I please be excused from this woman? Odin, forgive me, but I am way past the limit of my patience." Before the alpha could answer, Bolt walked out of the room.

Varg opened his mouth to say something but closed it again. He looked at Laney again. "What did you do to him?"

"Nothing," Laney answered. "I've been a perfect guest the whole day. If anything, he's the one who's lacking as a tour guide, refusing to answer even the simplest questions."

The tall woman's shoulders shook, and she snorted. She tried to cover it up with a cough but gave up and laughed out loud. Grabbing a piece of paper that Varg had in his hand, she strode over to where Laney sat. "I'm Nora," she said, "the pack's lawyer. Please look at this picture and tell me if you recognize anyone." She sat in the chair next to Laney's and handed over the sheet.

Laney looked at the striking blond couple in the image. "They look like twins. Who are they?"

"You don't know them?" Varg asked, watching her intensely. He'd walked over so quietly, she hadn't noticed him. Now, his muscular denim-covered thigh being right next to her face distracted her from the picture.

She had to look back down to remind herself of what the people looked like. "The woman is familiar." Laney studied the picture more closely. "But I can't place her. What's her name?"

"Inessa Novikov, but you may know her better as Inessa Butosova, her maiden name," Nora said.

Butosova was familiar, but not in a good way. "She's a dark witch. Like, very dark." Laney frowned. "And very bad news. The Witches and Mage Council has an entire team working on keeping magical artifacts out of her hands. But she seems to have unlimited resources to purchase them."

Varg nodded. “She's now married to the Russian-American alpha who commands the Eastern Packs Coalition. She and her brother are here on the west coast. We think one of them is your abductor.”

Laney looked at the picture again. “I don't think it was Inessa, but maybe the man. He is the right height and build. Inessa could have posed as male, though. I just have an impression of the person being an actual male.” She swallowed, not wanting to think about those hours she'd been hanging on the meat hook. “He kept distorting his features. So, it's only my gut feeling telling me it's a man. That and the fact that he had a broken nose. Every one of his shifting faces had that feature in common.” She looked back at the picture again and pointed at the guy's face. “This guy has a crooked nose.”

“I am almost certain Iakov is our guy.” Nora sounded excited. “Nick Novikov doesn't have a broken nose. At least not in the most current photos I could find online.”

A phone rang. Varg fished out a cell from his pocket and raised it to his ear. “Yeah.” He listened to the person on the other end and nodded a few times, and then his amused blue eyes caught Laney's gaze. “Justice wants to know what the combination is to the safe he found underneath the floorboards in your apartment.”

How the fuck had they found her hiding spot? She'd warded that location with an obfuscation incantation several times over. “I have no idea what you're talking about," she tried but knew she wouldn't get away with it as soon as the words left her lips.

"Did you hear that?" Varg asked into the phone. Nora had her hand in front of her mouth, and her shoulders shook again. The alpha wolf held out the phone to Laney. "He wants to talk to you."

She sighed but took the phone. "Hello?"

"You all right, luv?" a British voice asked, but didn't wait for her answer. "Just need to know if you want to give me the combination over the phone so I can open the safe here in the apartment. Or should I rip it out of the floor and take it to you? Trouble is, I may do a bit of damage if I have to move it." *Shit. Shit. Shit.* She tried to think of a way out of the situation, but there wasn't one. Varg watched her with a smile playing on his lips. She wanted to stick her tongue out at him. "Still there, luv?" the Brit, Justice she presumed, asked over the phone line.

"Look," Laney finally said. "You can't open it without me, and you can't move it without me."

"Pretty sure I can," the British voice said. "I'm extremely strong."

She sighed. The dumb wolf obviously thought brawn was the answer to everything. "I warded the safe with a kill incantation. If you try to open it without me present, or if you try to move it, you'll trigger the spell." The wolves were adversaries, but that didn't mean she wanted to cause their deaths.

Nora took a deep breath, and Varg growled.

On the line, the Brit just chuckled. "Clever girl. Well, you better get your smart arse over here and open it for me, then."

Laney handed the phone back to Varg. "This isn't over," she told him, but her heart sank. She'd lost her most substantial bargaining chip. But maybe she could still use the fact that the wolves didn't want anyone to know about the medallion's magical powers.

His eyes were cold as they met hers. "You almost killed my lieutenant."

She squared her shoulders. "No, I didn't. You almost killed him by telling him to snoop in my apartment without asking me for permission first."

"I don't remember you asking for permission when you stole the Odin medallion." He leaned over her, his eyes never leaving hers. The air crackled between them with anger and something more. Something delicious and sizzling.

The air suddenly felt too thick to enter her lungs properly. "What's so special about the medallion, anyway?" The words spilled out of her mouth on a breath of air.

Varg's pupils widened as he focused on her lips. Her lungs stopped working altogether.

Nora cleared her throat.

Varg blinked and took a step back. "Let's go," he said over his shoulder as he walked out of the room.

Laney shook her head and had to force her shoulders to relax before she could get up from the lounger. Nora shot her an amused look and then followed Varg.

That moment did not need to be repeated, ever.

If Stockholm syndrome was when a victim developed sympathy with their capturer's cause, what did you call wanting to jump your jailer's bones?

CHAPTER 10

Arek looked around Dr. Marconi's apartment. The devastation didn't look any different from the last time he had visited, but this time, the owner was with him. She'd seen the wreckage through the video feed that Bolt had shown her, but experiencing it in person would touch her emotionally. Her defiant behavior during their confrontation in the sunroom had disappeared as soon as they first walked into her wrecked home.

She'd quickly blinked them away, but he'd noticed the tears welling up in her gorgeous eyes as she looked around her destroyed home. He'd wanted to hug her, which was utter bullshit.

Arek didn't do cuddling. He did sex. The kind that left him and his partner exhausted and panting for more.

Hot, sweaty, sizzling sex without emotions.

Arek tried not to think that if Dr. Marconi had less of a conscience, his enforcer would be dead by now. It hadn't occurred to him or Justice, but of course, a witch would ward her hiding place. The pack was ill-prepared to deal with a regular magic practitioner. They would need a lot more training and a lot more information before confronting Inessa Novikov and her brother. He needed to convince Dr. Marconi to stay at the Pack House and help them prepare.

She walked through the apartment, her eyes wide and her arms wrapped around herself. Now and then, she'd stop and study something on the floor before continuing on her walkthrough.

Arek didn't want to rush her, but the longer they stayed here, the itchier he became. Sacramento's wolves could not locate the dark magic siblings' car, and the pair was currently not at their Modesto hotel. None of his wolves were safe until he knew where the dark magic siblings were.

Dr. Marconi had hidden her warded safe beneath the floor where her bed had stood before the two rogue wolves destroyed it. Arek wanted her in her bedroom, and not for any fun reasons, but she kept walking around the living space.

Justice cleared his throat. "You all right, luv?" he asked Dr. Marconi.

She took a while before she turned to face him. "Yeah," she finally said, gesturing toward the floor littered with debris. "I just didn't know it was this bad." She hiccupped, but then squared her shoulders. "Right, the safe." She finally walked toward the bedroom.

Justice moved to follow but stopped when Arek's wolf growled softly. The enforcer shot him a look. "What the fuck?" he mouthed silently.

Arek shrugged and stepped in front of Justice, so he'd be between him and Dr. Marconi. His wolf had never been possessive of women before, and he did not want to discuss why this little witch had caused such a reaction.

Dr. Marconi kneeled on the floor next to where Justice had pried open a square of the floorboards. A black iron door with a keypad and a blinking light rested below. "I'll open the safe," she said, "but I want your word that you will only take the medallion and leave the rest of the content with me."

Justice looked at Arek, one eyebrow raised. Arek nodded. "As long as there is nothing else inside the safe that belongs to a shifter pack, you can keep the content." He didn't add that neither Dr. Marconi nor whatever else was in the safe would stay in this apartment. The woman loved to argue about everything, so he'd leave this confrontation for later.

She placed both hands on the floor next to the hole and closed her eyes. The surrounding air shimmered, and the flooring underneath rippled in smooth waves. She didn't make a sound, yet Arek heard chanting and drums as if they came from very far away.

He looked over at Justice, but his enforcer was staring at Dr. Marconi, leaning forward as if she was pulling him toward her with invisible strings. Arek's wolf wasn't happy about that, but he ordered it to stand down. Magic thickened the air, and he wanted nothing to upset the spells Dr. Marconi weaved.

Her hands left the floor and twisted gracefully in the air. A stream of sand floated up from the safe, arranging itself in a thin stream that flowed into a pile on the floor, as if inside an invisible hourglass.

The sand stopped after a few minutes, and Dr. Marconi sat back on her heels. "All done," she said.

"What is that?" Justice pointed at the cone of sand. "Magical dust?"

Dr. Marconi smiled. "I'm an earthbound witch. My magic works best on non-manmade materials. Enchanting the metal of the safe would be too obvious to any other witch or a mage. Also, I couldn't figure out a spell that could effectively stop anyone from moving or opening the safe. So, I packed the hole with warded sand that did just that before lowering the safe into it.

"So, you made your own magical Semtex." Justice gripped the back of his neck and grinned. "Fucking clever girl. Can you teach me to do that?"

She tilted her head. "Do you have any earthbound powers? Do you feel drawn to certain rocks or trees?"

"Can't say I ever noticed anything like that, no." His enforcer shook his head.

Arek's wolf growled again.

Justice shot him another look. "But let's get on with it, then. Crack that safe open. My alpha wants his Odin medallion back around his pretty neck." The enforcer grinned at Arek.

Dr. Marconi keyed in a code, twisted the handle on the safe, and swung open the door on silent hinges. She reached inside and took out a black velvet pouch. Arek immediately felt the familiar pull of his medallion. She stood and walked over to him. "I'm sorry about taking this from you. I never would have if I'd known the claim you stole it was fake."

He nodded, took the pouch from her, and pulled out the artifact. It hung on a broken platinum chain.

"Oh," she said, reaching for the chain. When Arek instinctively swung it away from him, she cried out, "I can fix it."

He slowly handed it back to her. "Touch only the chain." She may have kept Justice from getting hurt, but that didn't mean he trusted her.

She rolled her eyes but did as he asked. Holding the two broken pieces of the chain together in one hand, she stroked a fingertip across the breakage, and the links of the chain twisted themselves together again. Arek studied the location of the break closely, but couldn't see anything different in that segment of the chain.

"Thank you," he said. Although why he expressed gratitude when she was the one who had broken the thing in the first place, he didn't know.

Dr. Marconi reached into the safe again and took out a small leather dossier. "Okay then." She looked at them expectantly. "I guess this is where we say goodbye."

Fat chance. Arek fastened the chain around his neck. "What's in there, and where are you going to go?"

She waved the small folder in the air and looked around the apartment. "Cash and my passport, plus an emergency credit card. I guess I'll stay at a hotel for a few days until I clean this up and get some new furniture." She looked around the space. "I'm not sure I'll stay here for long though, so it may just be some thrift store stuff at first."

Justice shook his head. "You're coming with us. Even if this place wasn't a wreck, you got two deranged dark mages and their mangy wolves coming after you."

Dr. Marconi paled. "But I don't have the medallion anymore. Why would they still want to hurt me?"

"They don't know that you don't have it," Arek said.

"And even if they did, they don't care," Justice added. "You got away from them before they could finish the job. You're a liability, luv."

"Finish the job?"

"Expire you. Make you unalive," his enforcer clarified. "They can't be sure you won't identify them and turn them in."

Her face turned even paler. "So, I was right. That meat hook was supposed to be my final destination." She glanced around the apartment again. "I'll have to lie low for a while, then. Maybe break my lease and get a new place."

Arek put his hand on her shoulder. "They'd still be able to find you, even if you left town. What you need is protection." He hoped she'd come to the correct conclusion on her own.

"I don't have anyone—" she stopped and swallowed. "I don't know how to—" she shook her head. "You want me to come back with you?"

"That's a great idea," Justice said, clapping his hands together. "Let's get the fuck out of here before them deranged siblings, or their wolves show up."

Dr. Marconi shook her head again. "No, I can't do that."

"Why not?" Arek asked at the same time as Justice said, "Where else are you going to go?"

"I can't just freeload off you. I need to get another insurance retrieval contract. Once I have some disposable cash, I'll have more options."

He sighed inwardly. Why did she have to make things so complicated? "You already have a great option. I already offered you a job."

She frowned. "You still want me to catalog your collection?"

"Of course." That and helping him prepare his wolves to take out the dark magic siblings. But that would be a later discussion.

She opened her mouth to say something, probably a protest of some sort, but Justice grabbed her shoulders and propelled her toward the door of the apartment.

Arek's wolf rumbled again.

Justice looked at Arek with raised eyebrows, but he dropped his hands. "That's settled then," he said. "Let's discuss the details on the way back to the Pack House." He grinned at Arek over his shoulder as he walked out of the apartment. "If I were you, Doctor, I'd negotiate a big salary with smashing benefits."

Great, now his enforcer represented the witch in employment negotiations.

Arek walked Dr. Marconi to her suite in the Pack House. She'd been quiet on the ride back, despite him trying to pull her into a conversation. "Are you all right?" he asked as they reached her door.

She shrugged. “I will be. The live experience of my destroyed apartment—my destroyed life—affected me more than I thought it would.”

He touched her shoulder and turned her around to face him. “Your life is not destroyed. Those were just things.”

Her amber eyes stared up at him, and her lips parted.

He couldn’t stop staring at her mouth. When her tongue darted out and touched her bottom lip, the wolf inside him growled in appreciation.

We like, the beast whispered to him.

She reached up and traced a fingertip across his lips. “Soft,” she whispered. “Just like I thought.”

Mine, the wolf roared. *Ours*.

Arek could no longer resist. He leaned down, his hand sliding from her shoulder. Careful of the wounds on her back, he gripped her right hip and pressed her against him. He buried his other hand in her glorious hair and crushed his lips against hers.

A moan escaped her lips, and he slipped his tongue inside her mouth.

Tasting, devouring.

Claim my mate, Wolf growled, the sound reverberating through Arek’s chest.

CHAPTER 11

Laney grabbed the collar of Varg's shirt, pulling him closer. His lips were soft but firm against hers. As his tongue danced with hers, every nerve ending in her body shuddered in delight. The sensation of his beard against her skin heated her core.

She laced her fingers behind his neck, pressing her core against his body. As she pushed her chest against his, the stiff peaks of her nipples rubbed against the sports bra, creating tantalizing friction against the fabric.

He growled into her mouth. The sound vibrated inside her, and she sighed her pleasure into his mouth.

Varg leaned her backward until her head rested against the door. He placed his hands on the wood so that they bracketed her head and pushed himself away from her. "If you don't want this, tell me now," he said, resting his forehead against hers, his chest heaving.

He grabbed the door handle by her hip. "Once I open this door and we step inside, I won't stop." Leaning back, he looked into her eyes, searching for an answer. "Decide now if you want to be mine."

She stared back. His irises turned ice-blue again. Caressing his neck with her fingertips, she tried to think logically. She wanted him so badly, but technically, he was a client now.

He kissed her temple and trailed his lips down to her ear. "Stop touching me, or I'm going to lose control." His hot breath caressed her neck, and she couldn't help but close her eyes and tilt her head to give him better access. "Marconi," he growled in warning.

A rough giggle escaped her lips. "I think we should start using first names."

"Elaine," he said, pulled down the collar of her t-shirt with his teeth, and nipped her collar bone.

Heat flooded between her legs. "Laney," she sighed. "Nobody calls me Elaine."

"Decide, Laney." He nuzzled her neck and then nipped her earlobe.

Her nipples were about to burst through the sports bra.

She couldn't sleep with a client. *Yes, you can*, her hormones shouted.

Screw it. She wanted him. And they hadn't signed a contract yet. Technically, he wasn't a client.

Rising on her tiptoes, she buried her fingers in his short hair.

She molded herself to his body and claimed his mouth with hers.

His tongue met hers thrust for thrust, and he grabbed her hip with the hand not on the door handle. "Are you saying yes?" he asked. "I need to hear it."

"Yes," she breathed into his mouth.

He groaned and swept his hand down her thigh. Hooking the back of her knee, he lifted her leg over his hip and pressed his hardness straight into her core.

Her panties dampened, and her breath quickened. "Open the damn door," she groaned."

Chuckling, he twisted the handle. As the door swung open, he pushed her through, turning her so that her back lightly pressed against his chest. As the door closed with a snick, he slid her panties and sweats down her hips. She stepped out of her shoes, socks, and clothes all at the same time.

He gripped her hips, pressing the bulge on the front of his jeans into the cleft between her bare buttocks. Her skin heated under his hands, and she arched her back. "I don't want to hurt your wounded back," he whispered.

"You're not," she gasped. "Earthbound witches heal quickly." Besides, the sensations he created in her body overpowered any pain her wounds might still experience.

With the tips of his fingers, he touched her damp pubic curls, and then slid his hand lower to bury a finger inside her. With the heel of his hand, he pressed against her mound.

White heat flickered on the inside of her eyelids as her core clenched around his finger.

His teeth scraped the skin on her neck, and then he bit her shoulder as a second finger joined the first.

Laney panted hard, trying to catch her breath. Her heart beat so fast it might jump out of her chest. "Varg," she moaned, gripping his wrist.

"Arek," he corrected. "We're on a first-name basis now, remember?" His fingers curled inside her wet core, and he tightened his grip.

She whimpered, pressing her butt back against him.

With a growl, he slipped his fingers out of her and grabbed the hem of her t-shirt.

She helped him pull it over her head and then grabbed the sports bra, which followed the shirt to land somewhere on the floor.

Arek paused for a moment, staring at her bare breast. His eyes lightened even further and when his gaze met hers, she could see something wild and feral peeking out at her.

He lifted her into his arms and hoisted her onto the bed. Watching her with fierce eyes, he grabbed the back of his shirt collar with one hand and pulled the garment over his head.

Laney bit her lip as she stared at his sculptured chest and abs. The Odin medallion rested against the fine blond hair that dusted his pectorals and then narrowed to a darker strip that disappeared into his jeans. "Pants too," she breathed out and locked gazes with him.

His pupils dilated, and a smile filled with male satisfaction played on his lips. "As you command." He unzipped the jeans and pulled them down with the boxer briefs underneath. As his erection sprung free, he stepped out of his shoes and socks.

Laney scooted backward on the bed to make room for him, but he caught her ankle and stopped her. "Not so fast," he growled. "I want to taste." Her brows furrowed as she tried to make sense of his words. A fraction of a second later, she had her answer as he kneeled beside the bed. He dragged her closer, positioning her butt right on the edge of the mattress.

Keeping eye contact, he draped her leg over his shoulders and lowered his face to her core. Feeling his hot tongue pressed against her clit, she cried out. A shock of white-hot pleasure shot from her center and spread through her body. Panting, she moaned Arek's name as she buried her hands in his hair, pressing herself against his mouth.

He lifted the other leg over his shoulder and pushed his hands under her butt. Tilting her pelvis, he buried his mouth so deep into her that his teeth scraped her clit. He sucked her hard as he pushed a thumb inside her.

Laney shattered. Wave after wave of heat shook her body, the pleasure so intense her hips shot off the mattress.

Arek tightened his grip on her buttocks and kept nipping and sucking the clit, swallowing her juices down as her climax pulsed for several moments.

His mouth didn't release her until she'd experienced several aftershocks.

Laney tried to say something, but her breath came in such short bursts that she couldn't form any words. She wasn't sure what she'd say, anyway. Thanks for the best orgasm, ever?

She giggled.

Arek wiped his chin with the back of his hand and smiled as he looked down at her. "I amuse you?"

"You amaze me," she breathed out, her body limp and sweaty against the bed cover. She pushed herself up on her elbows. "Let me return the favor."

He shook his head. "We're not done yet." Hooking one arm underneath her knees and draping the other around her shoulders, he climbed onto the bed with her in his arms. Half sitting down with his shoulders against the headboard, he positioned Laney on his lap and leaned down to kiss her deeply. "Ready for round two?" he said when she was once again panting and looking at him in a glazed-over stupor.

Her nipples ached for his touch, and she grabbed his hand and pressed her breast into his palm.

His pupils widened, and he kneaded her flesh, hard.

She twisted and straddled him. Leaning down to claim his lips with hers, she sucked his tongue into her mouth.

As she lowered her hips and took him inside her, Arek groaned loudly, releasing her breast to grip her hips.

She lifted herself and then sunk down again, taking all of his length this time.

The tip of his cock bumped against her cervix, causing just enough pain to push her pleasure over the edge.

He tilted his hands, and his fingers dug into the flesh of her buttocks. His tongue laved one of her nipples, and then his teeth nipped the sensitive peak before he sucked the whole areola into his mouth. Arek kept sucking and biting, driving her mad with desire.

Laney rode him faster, her hands on his shoulders for balance.

He squeezed her hips and buttocks harder, burying himself deeper inside her on each down stroke.

His mouth released one nipple and captured the other.

As he bit down on the hardened peak, Laney exploded.

Her back arched, and as she ground herself down so hard against him, she could feel his hip bones digging into the inside of her thighs. Her legs pressed against his, and her breath came in short bursts.

Arek released her hips, pushed her breasts together between his palms, captured both nipples with his mouth, and then gently bit down.

Another wave of climax shuddered through Laney's body.

As she cried out, he gripped her hips again and pumped inside her hard and quick.

She felt him erupt inside her, and as he found his release, he roared her name.

Laney collapsed, every muscle in her body limp. She leaned against him, waiting for her breath to slow down.

Arek pushed back her hair and bracketed her face with his palms. "Are you okay?" His eyes were deep blue again.

She nodded. "Very okay."

He scooted them both down and gently rolled her off him. Lying face-to-face, he played with her hair, tucking it behind her ear. "We didn't use protection," he said. "But humans can't catch diseases from shifters, and wolves can only impregnate their true mates."

"What does that mean?" she asked. "Bolt talked about that."

"True mates?"

She grinned. "Yes, I already know what impregnate means. Bolt didn't have to explain that to me."

He chuckled, tracing a finger down the side of her face. It seemed Arek Varg liked tactile contact. She didn't mind. She was a cuddler herself. "When shifters meet their true mate, their animal side claims them for life."

She raised herself on one elbow. "That's a very long time to be with a partner." Witches aged slower than regular humans, but shifters could live for centuries. "How old are you, anyway?"

He interlaced his fingers with hers and tugged. She fell against his chest. Pulling a blanket over them both, he said, "It's not polite asking a wolf his age, but for your information, I became a wolf in the early 1900s, when I was in my early thirties."

Dang. She'd just had sex with Grandpa Wolf. Not that she minded. He'd obviously picked up a trick or two to use in bed during the last century. She smiled against his skin.

"What are you laughing about?" he asked.

"Nothing," she said. "Just thinking about our age difference." She raised her chin so she could see his face. "I'm twenty-eight. You're robbing the cradle."

He smiled down at her. "Do you mind?"

"Not at all." She traced her finger around his nipple and watched it pucker. "I may have some questions for you, though, about history."

He captured her hand and brought it to his lips. "Of course, you do." He kissed her finger one by one and then sucked her thumb into his mouth.

Her core clenched, and her nipples tingled. "Round three?" she said half-jokingly.

He released her thumb, a wicked grin stretching his lips. "I thought you'd never ask." Apparently, being alive for more than a century had not tempered his stamina.

She was a very fortunate girl.

CHAPTER 12

Arek startled awake, trying to figure out where he was. The warm body draped over his chest helped him remember. Doctor Marconi—Laney—grunted in her sleep like a little cub. Someone knocked softly on the suite's door—again. That was the sound that had woken him.

He untangled himself gently from the sleeping witch and slid out of bed. Outside the window, pale tendrils of morning sun streaked the sky. Soundlessly, he padded on bare feet across the suite's sitting room to the door on the other side. "Yeah," he said in a low voice.

"It's Bolt. Sorry to wake you. But you need to see this."

"Give me a second." His second-in-command wouldn't have bothered him unless it was urgent. Arek pulled on his clothes and pulled the comforter over Laney before leaving the bedroom.

She mumbled something in her sleep, but he couldn't make out the words.

He joined his lieutenant in the hallway.

Bolt looked him over. "Was that wise? She's a witch." Unhappiness and anger traveled down the pack bond. What the fuck was this about?

"Not interested in your opinion," Arek shot back. "Why are you here?" He frowned. Justice, Bolt, and he were tight, but they didn't discuss each other's choice of bed partners. What did Bolt have against Laney? Arek had slept with witches before.

His lieutenant pushed his hands deep into his pockets. "Someone just called Justice about two dead wolves. They washed ashore on Kirby Cove Beach."

Fuck. "Drowning? Who are they?"

"I don't have the details. Justice drove down to confirm that they were indeed wolves. He called me and I came here to get you."

"Who found them?" If someone knew the body belonged to wolves, it was probably another shifter.

"The campground attendant is part of a local mountain lion clan. He recognized the bodies as shifters." Bolt rocked on his heels. "The campground has a few overnight guests. The lion wants us to get the bodies out of there as soon as possible."

Right. If regular humans got involved, it would get a lot messier. Dead bodies at a public campground would be hard to keep out of the press. "Let's go," Arek said, heading down the stairs to the first floor.

"I can meet up with Justice again and bring the bodies here," Bolt offered. "You should shower before we go. I can smell her on you." His nose wrinkled in distaste.

Arek stopped, took a moment to collect himself, and then stepped into his lieutenant's personal space. "What is your problem?"

Bolt started back. It took a powerful wolf to meet an alpha's stare. Both of his lieutenants were dominant enough to lead packs of their own, but so far, they'd never expressed an interest.

Commanding alpha wolves was a delicate balancing act. Arek dealt with it by encouraging them to express their opinions, but Bolt's behavior tonight bordered on disrespect. Arek's wolf growled his displeasure.

His lieutenant dropped his gaze. "No problem," he said. "None of my business."

"Let's keep it that way," Arek shot over his shoulder as they walked down the hallway to his suite. With Novikov's wife and her brother in his territory, he did not have time for a mutiny.

Not in his own house. And especially not led by someone he considered a brother.

Arek opened the door to his living quarters. He'd grab some clothes but would not shower. Bolt needed to know who was in charge. Besides, his wolf liked Laney's scent on them. Arek would think about what that meant later.

As THE CROW FLEW, it was only a few thousand feet from the Pack House to Kirby Cove Beach, but the Marin Headlands consisted mainly of rock formations and hills. Since they needed a car to transport the bodies in, they had to follow the serpentine roads for almost half an hour before meeting Justice. If they'd run as wolves, they'd arrived in only a few minutes.

The beach lay just below an old maritime artillery battery that hadn't been in service since the early 1930s. Because of the military building, a drivable road led down to the beach from the headlands. They parked the van by the battery and crossed the sand to where Justice stood next to a Caucasian man with sandy blond hair.

The man smelled like a mountain lion shifter and introduced himself as Peter Cavalier, the campground attendant. "Luckily, none of the campers are up yet," he said. "This bunch seems less interested in hiking or surfing. They spend most of their time hanging around their tents, drinking beer and smoking pot. They're not early risers, but that doesn't mean one of them won't wander down here at some point."

Arek shook his hand. "Thanks for calling us." He looked toward the surf's edge where two bodies lay and then met Justice's eyes. His enforcer moved his head a fraction of a millimeter—a minuscule head shake. For some reason, Justice didn't want him to ask the obvious question about who the two wolves were.

Cavalier looked up the hill to the campsite's location. "I'll head back up. If any of the campers are awake, I'll stall them." He crossed the sand and started on the walking trail that led to the campground. But Arek still didn't ask Justice about the identity of the wolves. Mountain lions had excellent hearing.

Instead, he crouched down by the bodies.

They'd been in the water for more than a day. The fish had already nibbled on them. Despite missing the tip of their noses and most of their eyes, he recognized them right away. They were the two men that had wrecked Laney's apartment. Novikov's wolves.

That's why Justice hadn't wanted to discuss their identity.

Fuck. Two dead rival wolves, just down the road from his Pack House. This could turn ugly. The last thing they needed was for other shifter clans to get involved in wolf politics.

As he stood, both Bolt and Justice looked at him with grim faces that probably echoed his expression. "There's a reason they someone dumped them so close to the Pack

House," Bolt said. He must also have recognized the bodies.

"It's a message," Justice echoed.

"Yeah, but what does it mean?" Arek asked.

"Doesn't have to have any deeper meaning than Novikov fucking with us," Bolt said.

Arek nodded. "I'm sick of that alpha messing around in my territory."

"This trouble all started with the witch," Bolt said bitterly.

Justice did a double-take. He patted Bolt's shoulder. "You all right, mate?" He frowned. "The witch stole the medallion, but Novikov set her up. She's not the cause of this problem. She's Novikov's target. Same as us."

Bolt shrugged. "I'll back the van up," he said, walking back up the beach to the road.

"What the fuck is his problem?" Justice asked.

"I have no idea," Arek said. "Let's load the bodies and get out of here before the humans wake up."

Justice walked on the other side of him, but then halted and grinned. "Now that I'm downwind from you, I think I know what Bolt's problem is. You slept with Dr. Marconi."

Arek frowned. "I've slept with witches before, and Bolt's never had a problem." Did his lieutenant have feelings for

Laney? Was that what this was all about?

Arek's wolf stirred. It didn't like anyone but them close to the sexy witch.

He hadn't noticed Bolt showing particular interest. Intense emotions, like desire, were hard to block from other wolves. As alpha, Arek especially would have picked up on Bolt's feelings through the pack bond.

"You rarely bring your conquests to the Pack House," Justice said as he lifted one body in a fireman carry. His nose wrinkled. "This fellow stinks." He grinned over his shoulder at Arek as he headed up the beach. "I think our little brother is jealous because Daddy has a new girlfriend."

Arek grabbed the other dead wolf, hoisted him over his shoulder, and followed his enforcer up the beach. "She's not my girlfriend. And I'm sure I've brought women to the Pack House before." But had he? He hadn't had a serious relationship in decades. But he must have brought a woman home before.

"Not to spend the night," Justice threw over his shoulder. "You prefer to sleep at their house so you can sneak out in the morning or leave if things get too emotionally complex." They'd reached the car, and he loaded the body into the open back of the van. Wiping his hands on his pants, he grinned at Arek. "I use the same trick, mate."

"What are you two chatting about?" Bolt asked.

"Nothing," Arek said as he dumped the body next to the other dead wolf. They did smell bad. The rot and decay lingered in the air. They'd require a lot of bleach to clean the van properly.

But Justice patted Bolt's shoulder. "We're discussing how to help you deal with your alpha having a girlfriend."

Bolt just grunted and went to open the driver's door.

"Not my girlfriend," Arek insisted, feeling ill at ease now. He must have brought home a date to the Pack House at some point. Just because he couldn't remember, didn't mean it didn't happen.

"You keep telling yourself that," Justice said as he opened the sliding door and jumped into the back seat.

Arek slid into the passenger front seat, next to Bolt.

Maybe he needed to make sure Laney didn't have any expectations beyond casual sex. Their time together had been spectacular.

Correction, explosive.

He definitely wanted a repeat experience, but he did not need a girlfriend. Emotions complicated things—made them messy. He had enough messes on his hands trying to lead the coalition, even when Novikov's wife was not running amok in his territory.

There was no room for additional complications in his life. And girlfriends made things complicated.

His wolf growled. *Not a girlfriend. Mate.*

Great, now the beast was obsessed with Laney. As if his life wasn't enough of a hot mess already.

The wolf was confused, though. Laney wasn't his mate.

The beast hadn't shown this kind of possessiveness before, but that meant nothing. With the worry and stress of Novikov infringing on Arek's territory, he'd just lost a little of the control he always kept on his wolf. That was all.

That had to be all.

CHAPTER 13

Laney left the shielded room in the basement and climbed the stairs to the first floor, where she headed straight to the kitchen. She'd spent the morning organizing Varg's—Arek's—collection. As she'd requested, the room now had a top-of-the-line laptop resting on an adjustable glass and chrome desk. Someone had also arranged for several large sacks of salt and a water-filled aquarium big enough to house a shark.

If she came across an item infused with dark or ancient magic that had grown out of control, which the Witch and Mage Council had named wild magic, she'd hopefully be able to null its effects inside a warded salt circle.

As a last resort, she'd dump it into the tank of saltwater. But then she'd damage the artifact and lose a priceless historical record forever.

Speaking of lost things, she hadn't been able to track down the alpha of the house all day.

She'd woken up alone, which was a bit of a disappointment, but also a relief since mornings after could be awkward. She blushed, thinking about how she'd fallen asleep after Arek had given her a fourth orgasm.

He'd certainly learned a few tricks during his many years of living. Her stomach growled, and she shook her head to stop thinking about sex and concentrate on a different type of hunger.

Bolt had shown her the kitchen briefly during their tour, but she'd forgotten its vast size. The chef who cooked the evening meals didn't arrive until the afternoon. Bolt had told her everyone in the house foraged for lunch on their own, and the morning chef often left sandwiches or meat platters in the fridge. He'd told her to help herself. The words had been polite, but his tone gruff.

It was weird to be disliked by someone on sight. Hopefully, it was just his prejudice against witches and not anything personal. Not that she needed Bolt—or any of the other wolves—to be her friend. She'd do the job Arek had hired her for. As soon as the pack had eliminated the problem with the evil siblings, she could move on with her life. Of course, the job in the basement would take some time, and she didn't mind working at the mansion. But she needed her own space.

But maybe she'd spend the night now and then to for some more amazing sex with Arek. But that was all.

She wasn't emotionally involved with any of the wolves. *Liar,* a voice whispered in the back of her mind.

Ignoring it, she placed the notebook she'd brought with her on the counter and opened one of the industrial-sized refrigerators, hoping today's lunch treat would involve sandwiches.

As much as she liked meat, an entire meal of just protein was a little too much. The goddess must have heard her wish, because she found a plate of turkey and Swiss on rye inside the fridge. Her favorite.

She tore off a sheet of paper towel from the dispenser on the counter and grabbed a sandwich. After only three tries, she found the cabinet that held glasses and filled one with tap water. She then brought the food and the notebook through a pair of double doors to the dining room.

Eating in the sunroom would be fabulous, but she wanted to get some work done, and that would not happen with the spectacular view on display.

As she munched on her sandwich, she opened her notebook and grabbed her pen. She'd hoped to start cataloging the artifact collection right away, but it was in such disarray that she didn't even know where to start. The items had been placed on the shelves haphazardly, with no regard for their function, age, or origin.

For a few minutes, she contemplated just putting them all in an enormous pile in the middle of the room, so she'd have empty shelves with which to start.

She'd found the ledgers that Arek had talked about, but they didn't seem to follow any order, either. They were mostly a bunch of scribbles that supposedly described an item, but most of the wordings were so vague they could refer to several articles. Arek, or someone else, had described one item only as "knife."

Considering she'd so far counted more than a hundred blades, daggers, and sickles, the entry was less than helpful.

There had even been a few scalpels. She shuddered.

Historical medical tools were not for the faint of heart. And if they were infused with magic, they were even worse. The difference between torture and ancient surgical procedures was very subtle.

Laney scribbled in her notebook, creating categories in which to sort the collection.

Should she go by origin? Purpose? Maybe the strength of their power? She'd have to ask Arek what system made the most sense to him.

Thinking about the wolf made certain parts of her body tingle. Parts that were a little sore, but she didn't mind. She should have an ethical problem about sleeping with someone she worked for. However, after last night, she'd make her principles stand down because there was no way she was passing up having sex with Arek again. There could, of course, be nothing more serious between them. She didn't do relationships.

She'd had a few casual boyfriends, and then there'd been James. A fellow academic and just as passionate about magical artifacts as her.

Laney had thought he might be the one. But he'd dumped her as soon as her graduate student had accused her of sexual harassment. Falsely accused her.

James hadn't even asked about her side of the story.

She shook her head. That was in the past and not something she'd dwell on now. It had taught her a valuable lesson. She should be grateful for that.

As long as she and Arek enjoyed exploring each other's bodies, they could continue sleeping together. Eventually, one of them would get bored, or she'd be done with the catalog project. She paused in her scribbles, more likely the former.

The double doors from the kitchen flew open, and Nora entered. "Hey," she said, striding up to the table. "Just the person I'm looking for."

"Here I am," Laney said, stretching out her arms.

The lawyer smiled and sat down on the opposite side of the table. "You said the Witch and Mage Council spend many resources keeping Inessa from acquiring magical artifacts?"

Laney nodded. "I don't know the details, but she's on the council's blacklist. Theoretically, auction houses and brokers are not supposed to sell to people on the list."

"Okay," Nora tapped on the tablet she'd brought. "I have this idea about why Inessa and her brother are here, other than to fuck with the pack, of course." She turned the screen toward Laney. "There's a big benefit dinner and an auction in Sarasota later this week."

Laney looked down at the tablet. A newspaper article described a children's charity benefit, ending with a paddle auction of historical items donated by private collectors. It didn't say specifically that the artifacts were of the magical kind, but reading the list of donors, it seemed likely. "This is the kind of auction where someone like Inessa might be able to nab a few items," she told Nora. "If I was blacklisted, this is where I would shop." Nobody could ban someone from attending a benefit. And then a few wads of cash could pass hands and that someone could also bid on the auctioned items.

Nora grinned big. "Excellent. Then all I have to do is get an invitation."

"Why not just tell the Witch and Mage Council that the siblings are likely to be at the auction?"

The lawyer tilted her head. "And what will they do other than try to stop them from buying artifacts? Inessa and Iakov broke pack laws. We must deal with them, or Arek loses respect as alpha. Besides, this is a shifter matter, not a council matter."

"Okay, then what will you do once you get to the benefit? Can shifters counteract dark magic?" She wasn't being facetious. She wanted to know if the wolves had a secret weapon against dark magic.

"I'm not going," Nora said. "The invitation will be for you and Arek, with Justice and Bolt as backup."

Laney blinked. "Come again?" No way she'd attend the benefit. It would be crawling with her former colleagues. James would probably be there too.

The lawyer stood. "I've already cleared it with the alpha and have arranged for a dress and accessories for you." She powered down the tablet screen and tucked the device under her arm. "We don't want people to know about the collection in the basement, so Arek will pretend to be your boyfriend, and you'll pretend to represent a wealthy collector who wishes to remain anonymous."

"Do I have a say in this?" Laney asked, her voice wobbling a little. "Shouldn't you clear this with me?" She may work for...consulting for the pack alpha, but she hadn't signed up for confronting a dark witch and her dark mage brother. Because they were siblings, they probably enhanced each other's magic. And if Iakov was the man who'd flogged her in the storage facility, she did not want to meet him again.

"I'm sorry," Nora sank back down into the chair. "That was insensitive of me. Of course, you have a say in this. Talk it over with Arek."

"Where is the alpha?" Laney asked.

"They found the two wolves who ransacked your apartment dead this morning, washed ashore not too far from here. Arek, together with Justice and Bolt, is trying to figure out what killed them."

"Not drowning then?"

Nora shook her head. "There's no water in their lungs and not a mark on their bodies."

Great, two dead bodies, killed under mysterious circumstances. That didn't sound like a dark ritual at all. "Poison?"

The lawyer studied her for a beat. "Would you be able to tell what killed them if it was through magic?"

Laney studied her hands. Probably. But that didn't mean she wanted to examine the bodies. She swallowed. "Most likely."

Nora stood again. "Please come with me."

Dark magic left a foul stain on its victims long after the sacrificial ceremony. Non-practitioners were usually not affected, but anyone who wielded powers had to be careful. This consulting gig was already way more complicated than Laney had expected.

And she wasn't even including that she wanted to continue sleeping with the client.

CHAPTER 14

They'd started with the bodies in the shed in the backyard. They stank so horribly, though, that Justice insisted they drag the folding tables outside and examine the dead wolves there.

"Is it my imagination, or are they decomposing faster than normal?" Arek asked. "Or is it just the smell that's getting worse?"

Justice held an arm in front of his face. "I don't know, but their rankness is worse than thirty minutes ago. Aren't you supposed to get used to foul smells after a while?"

"When will the doctor get here?" Bolt asked. Although not technically a medical examiner, the pack doctor had performed autopsies before.

"She's not," Justice answered. "She's out of town for the next few days at some medical conference."

Arek sighed. They'd opened up one wolf to examine the lungs. They were dry. Assuming the two assholes had died the same way, neither of them had drowned.

Their next step had been the worst, investigating the body's surfaces for blunt trauma, weapon marks, and bullet wounds. The smell had been horrible, especially to their sensitive noses. They had found no clues of what killed the wolves. "I'm going to have to call the other alphas and let them know about this."

Bolt shook his head. "Don't. Let's go over them one more time. If you call the alphas without knowing what happened, they'll just speculate and create drama. None of it will be helpful, and it will suck up all of our time."

He wasn't wrong. But what other option did they have?

His wolf perked up. *Mate.*

As if he didn't have enough to deal with. He did not need his beast fixated on Laney, confusing great sex with a true mate bonding. And why was the dumb animal perking up now? He rubbed his chest, mentally telling the beast to stand down.

Ours, his wolf growled.

Justice shot him an amused look before focusing on someone over Arek's shoulder. "Hey," the enforcer said. "Step right up to the place of terrible smells. Nay, the place of the worst fucking smells you can imagine."

Arek turned around to find Laney and Nora walking toward them. His beast perked up even more.

The lawyer carried a big sack of something on her shoulder. "I've brought the witch who's currently staying with us. Maybe she knows something about what may have killed the wolves who worked for the dark magic practitioners." Sarcasm practically dripped from each of Nora's words.

"Great idea," Justice pointed at the sack on Nora's shoulder. "What else did you bring us, Santa?"

The lawyer dropped her load on the ground. "Salt, you barmy Brit."

Justice laughed and walked up to Laney. "I hope you can figure out what the hell killed these gits. We have no clue." He put his hands on her shoulder.

Arek's wolf growled loudly. Mine.

The three pack members stared at him. His wolf focused on Justice. *Mine*, it repeated.

The Brit grinned widely and lifted both hands, palms forward. He slowly stepped away from the witch. "Easy there, alpha beast. Everything's fine."

Laney's head swiveled back and forth between Justice and Arek. "What's going on?"

"Just male wolves having some testosterone overload problems," Nora said with a grin just as wide as Justice's. "They'll calm down in a minute."

Laney sent Arek a shy smile. "Hi."

Mate, his wolf repeated, almost purring. Arek cursed inwardly. He'd hoped he was wrong about his wolf claiming Laney, but the dumb beast thought she was their mate. Who'd ever heard of a witch being a shifter's true mate? Ridiculous.

Plus, the mating bond was something the beast and the human sides decided on together. The wolf was just obsessed with Laney because it had been a while since Arek had a bed partner.

Some of his thoughts must have displayed on his face because Laney quickly turned away from him, but not before he saw the hurt flashing in her eyes.

He didn't want her as his mate, but that didn't mean he wanted to cause her pain. He took a step toward her, but she ignored him.

"Right," she said to Nora. "We need a separate salt circle around each body. If they're warded or cursed, they may interfere with my abilities, or feed power to each other."

The lawyer hoisted the sack of salt, tore a small hole in one corner, and walked around each body until a consistent stream of white granules encapsulated each table in separate ovals.

As she closed the last circle, Bolt exhaled loudly.

The smell of the dead wolves decreased in intensity.

"Why didn't we think of that?" Justice asked.

Laney slowly walked around the body nearest her, the wolf whose lung they hadn't sliced open. She leaned closer, scrutinizing the ear. "What did you do with their clothes?"

"Burned them," Bolt said. "They stank."

"Did you go through their pockets first?"

"Of course," Arek said. "There was nothing inside any of them."

Laney nodded. "Empty pockets. Empty head," she mumbled.

"What does that mean?" Justice asked.

Nora shushed him. "Let her work."

Laney walked over to the almost empty sack of salt that Nora had deposited on the ground. She reached inside and covered her hands with granules. "I know little about dark magic," she said to Nora. "But I think the siblings cursed these bodies with an ancient spell."

"Do you know what killed them?" Arek asked her. He rubbed his chest again. The damn wolf kept prancing, wanting to touch Laney.

She shrugged. "Maybe. It's a long shot, but it's all I got."

"Go for it," Nora urged.

Laney took off her shoes and flexed her toes in the grass. She looked at Justice. "It might work better if you all take a few steps back."

Pissed off that she spoke to his second-in-command instead of him, Arek opened his mouth to say something, but then his wolf hissed.

Hissed, like a damn cat.

Nora and Justice exchanged a look, both grinning like idiots. Glad he could entertain them.

Bolt just shook his head and stepped back from the tables, but his face had lost some of the tension that had been there since the morning.

Arek joined his pack members a few paces away from the witch and the bodies. He knew his eyes flashed ice-blue because the damn wolf refused to stand down.

Laney widened her stance and closed her eyes. She twisted her head from side to side and rotated her shoulders. Inhaling deeply, she raised her hands hip-level with her palms facing the sky. Another breath, and she lifted them to shoulder level. She tilted her head back, facing the sky, and a light breeze ruffled her hair.

The slight air current strengthened into a gusty wind, whipping her long tresses around her face. None of it reached Arek or the wolves.

She stretched her hands higher, rotating them so her palms faced each other above her head. The wind died down, but the ground under her feet rippled. She opened her eyes and lowered her arms, hugging herself. Walking backward just outside the salt line, she circumscribed first one table and then the other.

Arek could see her lips moving, but he couldn't hear her words.

She moved her hands, cupping her shoulders, her arms crossed in front of her chest. Still walking backward, she followed a figure-eight path, weaving around the tables. She stopped, and two loud pops sounded like tiny fire-crackers.

Laney sunk to the ground.

Arek ran toward her. "I'm okay," she said as he reached her. "Just exhausted. Did it work?" She pushed off the ground to stand, and Arek cupped her elbow, helping her rise. When she swayed, he put his arm around her shoulders.

"If by 'working' you mean shrink these fellow's skulls. Then absolutely, it worked like...well, magic," Justice said.

Arek turned to look at the dead wolves. Their heads looked like large raisins.

"What happened to them?" Nora asked.

Laney pushed against Arek, but he kept his hand around her as she walked closer to the tables. "Empty pockets. Empty Minds," she said again. "It's from this weird rhyme little kids with magical abilities learn. I found an old stone slab a few years ago that had those words inscribed, but they were part of a dark magic curse."

"What does the curse do?" Bolt asked.

Laney hesitated and scrunched up her nose. "It took me a while to find that out, but I discovered an old manuscript that had the same spell and also described the outcome. Basically, it turns your brain and skull into a sludge that leaks out your ears."

Nora gagged.

"Are you saying Inessa or Iakov completely lobotomized these men?" Arek asked, cold anger growing in the pit of his stomach. These weren't his pack members, and he would probably have killed them when he caught them. But he'd made it an honorable death. An honorable fight. This was a pathetic and cruel way to die.

"Fucking zombies," Justice mumbled.

Bolt stared at the two bodies on the table, a glistening sheen covering his face. He turned and almost ran into the house.

Arek was glad he'd skipped lunch. The stench of the bodies had made him lose his appetite. He squeezed Laney's shoulders. "Are you okay?" he asked.

She nodded. "I just need to lie down for a while. This required more energy than I thought." She walked over to retrieve her shoes and then continued into the house without looking at him.

Arek sighed. He had to talk to her later, but for now, he had an unpleasant video conference to organize. He could only imagine how up in arms the coalition's alphas would be when he told him about dark magic turning wolf heads into dried husks.

CHAPTER 15

Two days later, Laney walked down the stairs, holding the hem of the exquisite aqua-colored dress Nora had bought for her. A pair of stiletto silver sandals hugged her feet, and she carried a matching clutch. The shoes' straps went above the ankle, which made them more comfortable to walk in. She'd still need to watch what she drank tonight, though. The three-inch heels would make it hard not to tumble even while sober.

Hopefully, Inessa and Iakov would behave civilized if they showed up tonight. If Laney had to run to get away from them, she'd be toast unless she ditched the shoes, of course. It would be a shame, however. They were so pretty.

She reached the middle landing, and when she turned toward the final set of steps, she saw Arek waiting for her at the bottom.

Laney had to stop and take a deep breath. Arek Varg, in a tailored tuxedo, was a sight to behold.

The coat's black starkness and the shirt's white crispness should have washed out his light skin and blond hair. Instead, they highlighted his face's sharp planes and gave the perfect canvas for his azure blue eyes to look even more intense.

Telling her hormones to stand down, Laney continued down the steps.

She hadn't seen him since the afternoon they determined what killed the two wolves. He'd traveled for the last few days to visit other pack leaders and take care of some business stuff. He hadn't told her the details.

She's missed him, which annoyed her. The collection had kept her busy during the days, but dreams of the alpha had filled her nights. Sizzling sweaty dreams.

Arek moved toward her, holding out a hand to support her. "You look amazing." Male appreciation shone in his eyes, which never left hers, despite the generous cleavage the dress put on display.

She took his hand and tried not to react to the heat that sizzled between them as their skin touched. "Thank you. Nora has the perfect eye for my size and what color would suit me."

"She didn't pick out the dress. Justice did," he growled.

Okay, so that was a little creepy. She didn't know the Brit had spent that much time cataloging her body. "I'll have to thank him," she said with an awkward smile, letting go of Arek's hand.

Arek must have picked up on her discomfort. "He takes one look at a person and instantly knows what would suit them. It's like a low-grade superpower." He gestured toward his outfit. "He picked this for me. I didn't even have to visit the tailor. It fits perfectly with the measurements Justice gave them."

Okay, that made her feel a bit better. She allowed herself one more perusal of the splendid form of Arek in the tux. "Well, he certainly picked out what would make you look good."

"Ah, so you're saying I'm good-looking tonight?" His eyes twinkled.

Oh, please. The man knew he was devastatingly handsome. "You clean up well," she said. He didn't need her to fan his ego.

"Shall we?" Arek gestured toward the door.

She nodded, and they walked out together, him holding the door open for her. A black limousine waited for them outside. Arek opened the back door and held her hand for support while she stepped inside. Following her, he kept supporting her as she lowered herself into the seat. The soft leather hugged her body.

As he sat, he turned to the driver. "Hey, it's your job to open and close doors."

Bolt turned to grin at them from the front seat. "Got it, boss."

Laney did a double-take. She'd never seen Bolt smile, and she'd never seen him dressed in anything but jeans or sweats. Tonight, he wore a dark suit, looking every bit like a driver who doubled as a bodyguard. He'd been in a much better mood ever since they figured out what killed the east-coast wolves.

She'd known Bolt would be their driver and that Justice would follow behind on a motorcycle, but she hadn't expected the limo.

"You went all out," she said to Arek as the long car rolled down the driveway.

"What kind of boyfriend would I be if I didn't spend my money to impress my date?" He lifted her hand and brushed his lips across it, barely touching her skin. His eyes never left hers, and when she shivered, a smile of male satisfaction graced his mouth.

The heat sizzling through her body from where his lips had touched her hand combined with her nerves became a sensation overload, and she quickly pulled her hand away.

Arek frowned. "Did I do something wrong?"

"Just nervous," she said. "I'm not good at pretending. Plus, there are going to be some people there that I haven't seen in a long time." She hadn't stayed in touch with any former colleagues from the university. Not that they'd reached out to her once the false accusations had forced her to resign. And if her ex showed up, which seemed likely since he managed the university's artifacts acquisitions department, she wasn't sure she could play her role.

Seeing him tonight, on top of pretending to date Arek, on top of hunting down Inessa, was a little much to deal with.

"Don't be," Arek said. "I will be by your side the whole night, and Bolt will be there to protect you too."

Their driver met her gaze in the rearview mirror. "Got that right," he said with another grin. She finally figured out why he was so happy. Bolt was looking forward to a fight.

"It's not that," Laney said. "I didn't leave the university on good terms, and some of my colleagues will be there tonight."

"That's what happens when you get caught sleeping with your students," Bolt chimed in. "You should have been more careful."

She bristled and straightened in her seat. "So, you're saying the sleeping part was okay, but I was stupid getting caught?"

Bolt nodded.

She looked at Arek. "What do you think?" His answer mattered more than it should, and it irritated her.

He held up his hands, palm facing her. "I don't know the particulars, so I have no opinion. Maybe you were in love with this guy, and the two of you couldn't wait until he was no longer in your class."

Laney shook her head. At least he kept an open mind, but she hated having this stupid scandal hanging over her head. Especially since it wasn't true. "I didn't sleep with my student. That would be unethical. Also, he wasn't in my class. I was his thesis advisor." She sighed. "He thought he deserved to graduate early, and when I disagreed, he accused me of making sexual advances. He told my department chair and dean that I wouldn't sign off on his thesis because he had turned me down."

"But if it wasn't true, that shouldn't have mattered," Arek said. "Once they investigated, they would have figured out that he wasn't ready to graduate. Once that was obvious, your reputation and work ethics should have made them support you."

Laney smiled wryly. "The university had recently lost a sexual harassment suit. And rightly so, because the faculty member involved was definitely guilty. So, they'd made a big deal in the media about passing a new policy that included starting any future investigations from the position of believing the victim." She brushed an invisible speck of lint off her knee. "The irony is that

I was the chair of the committee who created that policy."

Arek took your hand. "I bet you pissed off some people doing that. Not everyone responds well to change."

She nodded, taking comfort in how good her hand felt in his. "I did indeed. One of them was my department chair, with whom I'd had other disagreements as well." Her supervisor's betrayal still felt raw, even though it had been two years since the incident now. "He decided that my student's project *was* ready and that it meant his accusations had merits. As so often happens in these cases, the sexual harassment charges came down to my word against my student's, and in the end, they couldn't prove his case or mine."

"So why did you leave?" Arek asked.

"Because there was a stain on my reputation, which meant that most opportunities were now closed to me." She didn't add the derision and disbelief she'd received from former colleagues whom she thought were friends or that the classes she offered to her from then on were the ones nobody else wanted. Or that her research project's budget suddenly got cut.

But worst of all was James's betrayal. They'd talked about marriage. That was how in love she'd thought herself. How much she thought he loved her.

He'd dumped her the same night she found out her student would graduate after all.

Arek caressed her hand. "Well, tonight, you return triumphantly with a billionaire boyfriend at your side, representing a reclusive collector who trusts only your opinion about what to buy."

She smiled. Wouldn't that be wonderful? Not the boyfriend part. She was done with those and preferred to support herself, but rubbing her former colleagues' noses —especially James's—in how she now had access to a much more impressive collection of artifacts than what the university owned would be fantastic.

In a way, it wasn't so far from the truth. Even if they still hadn't signed a contract, she represented Arek. And he did have an extensive and impressive collection, even if it would take decades to sort out precisely what he'd acquired.

"What exactly were your plans for the items in the basement?"

He shrugged. "I didn't have a plan. I just acquired items that somebody could use against shifters and dumped them in the basement. Someone told me I should shield the room with thick lead, so I did."

"Where did you find the money to do all that?"

He raised her hand and nibbled on her fingertip. "Did you miss the part where I told you I'm a billionaire?"

"You were serious?" She knew he was wealthy, but a billionaire?

Arek laughed. "It's amazing what you can do on the stock market when your long game can last a century. Plus, the security company is doing well."

"What do you spend your money on?"

"The stuff in the basement." He smiled. "Seriously, most of the money is tied to the pack. There's a trust that makes sure every member is comfortable, regardless of income level. We've bought up a lot of land around the Pack House and created legal protections in case the state ever decides to sell off the public lands."

"That's a lot for Nora to take care of."

"She has a team of lawyers and paralegals that work for her, but most of the intricate details about how to protect our resources legally come from her brilliant mind." Admiration tinted his tone, and Laney felt a stab of jealousy, which was stupid because Nora was brilliant.

And Laney wanted nothing more from Arek than a good time in bed.

CHAPTER 16

A little more than an hour after they'd set off from the Pack House, the limo pulled up outside the Villa Montalvo in Saratoga. This time, Bolt remembered to get out and open the door.

Arek watched Laney gracefully slide out of the car and marveled at how she navigated the tall heels she wore.

He'd meant to talk to her about their relationship during the car ride, but she'd been nervous, and launching into a serious discussion about his wolf's obsession with her seemed an extra burden she didn't need this evening. And they'd only slept together once. The beast would calm down after they'd spent some more time in bed. He was sure of it.

He thought about what she'd told them about her resignation.

Arek wanted to punch her former department chair and dean. The possibility of one of them, or both, attending tonight plastered a grin on his face, but he'd promised Nora no public fighting.

The Western Packs Coalition also wanted the matter of Inessa and her brother handled quietly. They needed to deal with Nick Novikov and his raw ambition, but no evidence led to him directly. The alphas had debated the issue for hours, and no matter how they twisted the case and looked at it from all angles, Novikov could wrangle himself out of a formal accusation through one legal loophole or another.

The dead wolves could be rogues who acted on their own. That reflected poorly on their alpha, but it happened. Inessa and her brother could be sightseeing in California.

Yes, as the spouse of an alpha, Inessa should have asked permission before entering the Western territories. However, as a non-shifter, she could claim ignorance of the rules, or at least claim they didn't apply to her.

The debate over legal minutia had driven him nuts. Thinking about this night with Laney kept him from blowing up during the meetings more than once. This was his reward for suffering through all of that. A beautiful woman on his arm as he sized up his enemy and hopefully got to punch them at least once. Out of the public eye, of course.

They walked through the villa and onto the back terrace where wealthy patrons dressed in designer labels mingled and drank champagne. Saratoga, a small community southeast of San Francisco, had the honors of qualifying as the country's most expensive suburb several years in a row. It made sense that this place hosted an exclusive magical artifact auction.

Most of the collectors could walk home at the end. The organizers marketed the event as a benefit, but Nora had done her homework and discovered that everyone counted the auction as the major attraction. The benefit provided an opportunity for the non-profit not to have to follow standard magical artifact regulations, since it was all for charity.

He tucked Laney's hand under his elbow as they ascended the broad steps up to the terrace. She smiled at him, and he wanted to kiss her. The wolf's infatuation messed with his head. He needed to sort himself out if he were to hunt down the dark magic siblings.

Bolt and Justice had melted into the shadows, serving as a backup if needed. They counted on the dark practitioners not wanting a public spectacle. He wouldn't say he expected them to cooperate when he confronted them, but he did expect them to leave his territory and stop fucking around with his pack.

Laney took a deep breath before stepping onto the terrace.

"If Iakov is the man who abducted you," Arek said. "I will deal him with tonight. You don't have to worry about him anymore."

She flashed him a shaky smile. "Whether or not he is that man, I'm not looking forward to meeting him."

A server approached with a tray of champagne. Arek grabbed a glass for them each. "You don't have to drink it," he said as he handed the sparkly beverage to his date. "But it helps to have something to do with your hands."

She laughed genuinely at his lame joke, a lovely sound that did weird things to his insides.

A tall slim man behind her turned around, and when he saw the source of the joy, his face lit up with recognition. "Laney," he exclaimed, and when she turned around, he pulled her into a hug.

Arek's wolf growled, maybe out loud, because his date gave him a startled look. The strange man finally stopped hugging her, but rubbed her shoulders as he held her at arm's length. "You look amazing."

She did, but that wasn't any of this damn guy's business. Both Arek and the wolf agreed on that. They growled again, deep down in their throat. He put down both of the champagne glasses on the terrace railing.

Laney extracted herself from the man's grip. "Thank you, James...oh." She stumbled a little as Arek grabbed her hand and pulled her to his side. As she found her balance, she smoothed down her skirt with her free hand, trying to free the one in Arek's grip, but he held on. She shot him a look and cleared her throat. "Have you met Arek Varg?"

The man shook his head. "No, I haven't." He smiled, but the expression didn't reach his dark eyes. Arek didn't even bother. He just returned the man's chilly gaze with his alpha stare. "You date shifters now?" The man's lip curled.

Laney ignored the man's comment and continued as if Arek's wolf's angry, low growl didn't vibrate deep in his chest. She turned to him, a fake smile on her lips. "Arek, this is James Finley. We used to work together at the university."

Finley proved to be a stupid man because, instead of turning around and walking away, he said, "We were a lot more than that, Laney." His eyes never left Arek's as he chuckled without mirth. "We were about to get married."

His date shook her head. "I wouldn't go that far."

"You may not have worn my ring yet." Finley frowned. "But we talked about it."

"Did we?" Laney tugged on her hand in Arek's grip again. He held on. "That's not how I remember it." She waved her free hand in the air. "It's all a long time ago now." A sweet smile played on her lips.

Tug, tug.

Arek kept holding.

The man smelled like Laney, but spicier. A mage. "Nice to meet you." Arek pulled Laney closer, draping his arm over her shoulders without breaking eye contact with Finley. His witch muttered something under her breath. It sounded like "testosterone," but he couldn't be sure and didn't catch the last part.

The man's eyes narrowed as he looked at Arek's arm, cradling Laney. "Are you a collector, or just here to give away money?" he asked Arek, taking a sip out of his glass.

"No," he answered without specifying which question he addressed.

Laney rolled her eyes. "His role is to be eye candy tonight," she said sweetly. "I'm here to bid on my client's behalf."

Finley quirked an eyebrow. "Eye candy? Sounds like a miserable job."

Arek shrugged and picked up one of the champagne glasses. He took a sip.

Horrible stuff. The bubbles made the wolf sneeze, but Arek suppressed the sound. "The benefits are significant." He smiled at Laney, who rolled her eyes again. He ignored her and kissed the top of her hair.

"We should mingle," Laney said with a small laugh, but a tic spasmed in her jaw.

"Who's your client?" Finley asked.

"She can't say," Arek answered. "Confidentially agreement."

"So you don't know either."

"I know." Arek took another sip of the vile liquid in his glass and resisted the impulse to spit it out. A server passed by, and he placed the half-full glass on his tray. "I'm friends with the client." He brushed his lips against the top of Laney's hair again. "My friend introduced us." His witch muttered something under her breath. He couldn't hear any part of what she said this time, but the tone conveyed enough of the message.

"Do you have an eye on something special going up for auction tonight?" Laney asked Finley.

The man smiled at her. "I wouldn't tell you if I did. I know how competitive you are." He looked back at Arek. "This lady is cutthroat. Even after we were engaged, she'd go after every promotion, every research grant that I wanted."

"Must have been hard for you to keep up," Arek said.

Laney laughed genuinely. "It was."

"Well, at least I'm not the one who had to resign from my position at the university," Finley said petulantly. So, not just a loser, but a sore one.

Laney's face clouded over. Hurt flashed in her eyes.

Arek wanted to punch Finley, but figured it would draw too much attention. Instead, he tipped Laney's face up with his knuckle under her chin and bent down to kiss her. He kept it chaste, no tongue, but left his lips on hers for just a moment too long. "Their loss, my gain," he said without breaking eye contact with the sexy witch. "If she hadn't left, my friend wouldn't have hired her and introduced us."

She smiled at him.

Finley cleared his throat. "I should get going."

"You should," Arek agreed. Go, his wolf growled.

"Good to see you, James." Laney's tone belied the words.

"Save me a dance?"

"No," Arek said. This guy needed to give up. Now.

Finley opened his mouth, but then closed it again. He nodded to Laney and glared at Arek, who gave him the alpha stare back, knowing the wolf had turned his eyes icy-blue. The asshole caught the drift because he quickened his step as he departed.

"Was that necessary?" Laney asked, trying to shrug out of his hold around her shoulders.

"Yes," Arek said. "That guy is an ass."

"I agree, but you can't get into a pissing contest with every asshole you meet."

Could too, but he kept that to himself. Instead, he swung her around so he could kiss her properly. She'd probably continue the argument later, but it was an effective way to distract her for now.

CHAPTER 17

Laney shook her head once Arek stopped kissing her. "Sometimes, I'm just so happy I don't have to deal with testosterone overload."

Although she'd enjoyed certain parts, the pissing contest between Arek and James had been ridiculous. Since they'd never met before, Arek must have instinctively pushed all the right buttons to set James off. Maybe all alphas knew how to do that.

"I'm happy you don't have testosterone overload as well," he shot her a sexy grin. This man confused her. How could she be delighted with him one moment, only to be infuriated by him the next? The emotional rollercoaster exhausted her, although her hormones knew precisely what they wanted.

This alpha wolf, all the time.

"What was with the growling?" she asked. The sound had reverberated deep inside her, and at first, she thought James had experienced that too, but her ex didn't react if he did, so she'd kept her reaction hidden.

Arek scratched the back of his neck, his collar shifting, offering a glimpse of the platinum chain around his neck. "About that..." he trailed off. His head snapped up. "Bolt's in trouble."

He grabbed her hand and dragged her behind him as he weaved between the people milling around on the terrace.

"I didn't hear anything." She had to jog to keep up with him. Grabbing the skirt of her dress, she lifted it so she wouldn't trip.

"The pack bonds," Arek said. "I feel his distress through the pack bonds."

They reached the corner of the terrace, and the alpha continued down the steps onto the lawn.

Laney's heels sunk into the grass. "Hold on," she sighed. "I have to take off my shoes."

Arek held her hand while she balanced on one foot and then the other, slipping off the sandals. His nostrils flared as he scented the air, eyes flashing icy-blue. As soon as she'd gathered the shoes in one hand, he grabbed the other and took off again.

Soon, they arrived at the edge of the lawn where the light from the terrace didn't reach. Arek continued straight into the glade of trees surrounding the grounds. Darkness clung to the trunks, and debris like leaves and branches littered the ground, making it hard for her to keep up in her bare feet. She stumbled and stubbed her toe, a small "ouch" escaping her lips.

Arek turned just as a cloud cleared the moon, and pale light illuminated his face. His eyes glared icy-blue, and he tilted his head as he watched her. Something wild peaked through in his gaze. "Mate," he said with a low growl, and she knew his wolf spoke through him.

Mesmerized by the intensity in his eyes, she held her breath. Slowly, she reached up to cup his face. He leaned into her touch. A sound almost like a deep purr vibrated in his chest, and she felt it echo in her own.

Suddenly, his head snapped up and his nostrils flared. "Bolt," he said and looked down at her again.

Before she had a chance to react, he hoisted her into a fireman's carry and took off again. The ground rushed by underneath her face as she hung upside down, draped across his shoulder. His arm looped over her thighs while the hand kept a firm grip on her butt. If the blood rushing to her head hadn't made her so dizzy, she'd admire the effectiveness of the position and how skillfully he anticipated when she'd bounce as he ran through the trees, leaping over fallen logs and low snarly undergrowth.

The terrain shifted to a hillier landscape, and she guessed they'd entered the green belt of the El Sereno Preserve, adjacent to Villa Montalvo.

They entered a clearing where Arek slowed down and finally stopped.

He lowered her to the ground, his gaze on her face as he did. "Are you okay?" he asked, tucking a loose tendril of her hair behind her ear. "I'm sorry. I had to get here quickly."

He'd just run several miles, and yet his breath hadn't changed. Meanwhile, she panted heavily, and from the strands of hairs obscuring her view, she knew the elaborate hair updo that Nora had helped her with had collapsed. "It's okay," she said. "I understand." A pack member had called him through their bond, and his wolf had responded.

"I couldn't leave you unprotected." His azure blue gaze bore into hers. Arek had control of the wolf again.

She nodded. "I know. I truly understand." She looked around the clearing. "Where's Bolt?"

A man stepped out from the trees on the opposite side. "He had to leave." He walked further out into the grassy meadow, and Laney saw his face more clearly as the moonlight illuminated his features. Iakov Aslanov.

She recognized him from the picture, and when she reached out with magic to sample his power, she identified it as the same as that of the man who'd abducted her. Her chest tightened, and her breath hitched.

Arek took her hand and pushed her behind him. "Where did Bolt go?" he asked.

Iakov shrugged. "He didn't say." He kept walking toward them. The smile on his lips sent chills down Laney's spine.

Something in Arek changed. His posture remained the same, but she sensed a new intensity in him. From behind his back, she couldn't see his face, but she bet his eyes were now icy-blue. The wolf had come back out.

Iakov must have noticed, too, because he hesitated for a beat before continuing his walk toward them. A few feet away, he finally stopped. He leaned to the side so he could peek around Arek and meet her gaze. "Hello again, my little witch."

Arek's wolf growled, and he sidestepped to block the mage's view of her.

Happy that she'd already removed her shoes, Laney curled her toes into the dirt, connecting with Mother Earth. She reached out with her senses, searching for a ley line of power.

The chilly smile on Iakov's lips widened. "Ley line magic," he said. "How quaint."

Screw him. Laney tapped into the ley line she found running through the green belt. Its power flooded her senses, and she filled up the reserve she had inside her for exactly this purpose.

This magic worked differently than when she connected with different dimensions. She'd learned this ritual when she went to mage school. She'd asked her teachers about the bending of dimensions, but none of them understood what she'd tried to explain. When she'd shown them, they wrote it off as a cheap party trick, so she stopped asking questions and focused on the lessons about traditional magic-wielding instead. She'd mastered the discipline and graduated at the top of her class, but that didn't mean she stood a chance against a dark practitioner.

Arek stepped further into the clearing, facing off against the mage. "What do you want?" he asked.

"I want my witch back and your pelt to round out my collection of western pack rugs," Iakov answered.

Laney gasped. Had he killed Bolt and Justice?

No, Arek would have felt it through the pack bounds and said something.

"Not going to happen," Arek growled.

"You don't have a choice," Iakov countered. "My sister has immobilized your wolves, and there's nothing you can do about me claiming my witch."

Arek struck lightning fast. One moment, he stood next to Laney. The next, he slashed the mage across the face with his hand, now shaped like a claw.

Deep gashes marred Iakov's face, and blood trickled down his cheek. He swiveled as Arek threw an uppercut that glanced off the mage's cheekbone instead of landing as a solid blow.

Arek crouched low and swept out with a back kick, but Iakov parried with magic.

His eyes blazed as he extended his arm, power shooting from his fingertips.

Laney recognized the signature of the magic as what he'd used when he whipped her and grew tired of using the leather tool.

She screamed as Arek took the blast head-on and fell to the ground.

Iakov turned to her. "Just you and me now, little witch."

Out of the corner of her eye, Laney saw Arek's leg twitch and his chest rise and fall.

He'd been stunned, not killed.

She exhaled in relief but kept her eyes on Iakov so he wouldn't look at Arek.

The mage walked closer with gliding, menacing steps.

Laney widened her stance. She probably had only one shot. It would most likely not work, but maybe she could weaken the mage enough to where Arek could finish the fight.

Behind Iakov, the air shimmered, and a gray wolf stood where Arek had lain. A pile of clothes lay in the grass beside him.

"I know you shifted," Iakov said, tilting his head to the side but not breaking eye contact with Laney. "Your beast won't protect the witch any better than your human form. She's mine to do with as I wish."

The wolf snarled. Its lips curled and pulled back from sharp teeth that glimmered in the moonlight.

Iakov turned around to face the wolf and then threw back his head, laughing loudly. "Aw, the beast has sharp little teeth. Isn't that cute?"

Laney pulled more power from the ley line. She'd already taken too much, and dizziness clouded her vision.

The wolf stopped snarling and looked at her.

Mate?

The question whispered through her mind as Iakov raised his hands, his eyes intent on the wolf.

As he released his power, Laney screamed and pushed all the power she'd stored inside herself into an assault on Iakov.

She then opened herself as a conduit with a direct connection to the ley line. Something she'd been taught repeatedly never to do, because it fried the practitioner. But she couldn't think of any other way to stop a dark magic mage.

Mate.

The scream echoed loudly inside her head as a bright white light exploded inside her eyelids, and she lost consciousness.

CHAPTER 18

Arek came to naked and cold, lying on a rough cement floor. His head hurt like hell, and the rest of his body ached too. With a groan, he pushed off the floor and tried to stand. The world tilted, and the floor rose to smack him in the face. Before it made contact, arms grabbed him and lowered him until he sat solidly on his butt again.

The rim of a water bottle touched his lips, and he gobbled the liquid down.

"Easy, boss. You're going to make yourself sick."

He opened his eyes to find Bolt bottle-feeding him as if he were a cub. Arek grabbed the bottle so he could drink by himself. But he took smaller sips because his stomach cramped, proving Bolt right.

"Glad you could join the party, mate." Justin mock saluted him from across a small square concrete cell. Both he and Bolt were as naked as himself. Not that he minded. Shifters were often naked together and didn't share the same hang-ups about bodies needing to be clothed that humans seemed to have.

Non-shifters seemed always to sexualize unclothed bodies. To shifters, it was just a state of not wearing fur. Although Arek preferred not to have to fight naked, and since he was in enemy territory, some covering would have been nice.

"What the hell happened?" Arek's voice sounded like gravel, and it hurt to talk. He touched his chest, looking for the familiar feel of cold platinum. Fuck, the medallion was gone.

"Don't know," Bolt answered. "I walked the perimeter of the party and then shifted so I could survey the whole parkland around the villa quicker. One moment, I'm running through the park. The next, I wake up here with the worst hangover."

Arek looked at Justice and quirked a brow. Words hurt too much.

"Very similar to my story." His enforcer shrugged. "I powered off my motorbike and shifted to wolf to examine the vehicles in the parking lot for scents of dark magic. Next, I know, I wake up here with Bolt." He pointed at Arek. "You look a lot worse than how I felt when I regained consciousness. What the fuck happened to you?"

He had to think for a while before the events came to him.

Iakov, in the clearing.

Laney was there too.

He tried to stand again, but the floor tilted again, and he had to sit back down. "Laney," he said. "Where's Laney?"

Bolt and Justice exchanged a look. "We don't know," Bolt said. "This cell is soundproof. So, we have no idea where we are or what's outside. We haven't even found a door. You just appeared in here."

No Laney, no medallion. He tried to think, but the pounding in his head kept getting worse. "Laney and I fought Iakov. She did something." He rubbed his temples. "Fuck, I don't remember the details. I think she blasted him with magic, but I don't know. He knocked me down, so I shifted, but that's all I remember." Arek stood, and this time he remained upright by bracing a hand against the wall. "I abandoned her with Iakov. Last time, the asshole whipped her to shreds. What if she's hurt? Worse, what if she's...." He couldn't finish the sentence. Couldn't even think about Laney not being in the world.

She belonged with the living.

She belonged with him.

He swayed again.

"Hey, calm down." Bolt rushed up to hold his shoulder. "I'm sure she's fine. The little witch is resourceful, and she's survived Iakov once. She can do it again."

Arek turned and leaned his back against the wall. He couldn't stomach sitting down again. The cool cement felt better against the back of his head and shoulder than the chilly floor did on his butt. "She shouldn't have to face him alone again. She's fears him." In the clearing, he'd felt how scared she was. He rubbed his chest.

"She told you that?" Justice asked, his gaze intense. "Or you felt it?"

"She didn't tell me. I just knew." He frowned. "I mean, it would make sense that she was scared, right?"

Bolt swore under his breath. "I'm sure she's fine," he muttered. "Look, whoever has us trapped here obviously wants us alive. Otherwise, they wouldn't give us this." He held up his water bottle.

Justice turned toward Bolt. "You know that's not my point."

Bolt just shook his head.

"What is your point?" Arek asked.

"We joked around about your wolf claiming Laney, but then it happened," Justice said. "If you can feel what she feels, the wolf's made her your true mate."

"No," Arek shook his head. "I mean, he's infatuated with her, but the wolf doesn't just claim a mate. It has to be a joint decision between the beast and the human." He looked between Justice and Bolt. "Doesn't it?"

“Don't look at me.” Bolt clenched his fists. “I have no idea how true mating works. Especially not with a witch.”

“Fuck.” Justice said. “Why are you so hung up on her being a witch?”

Bolt just shrugged. Apparently, today was the day he wanted to save all his words.

Justice turned back to face Arek. “I knew nothing about shifters—other than that I was one—until you saved us from the pits.” Arek started to say that he hadn't saved them, just killed the bastard that kept them prisoner. The pit master needed killing because he forced people to become wolves against their will and then exploited them. Finding Bolt and Justice had been a bonus. But his enforcer waved a hand before Arek had a chance to say all that. “Yeah, I know you don't think of yourself as our savior, but you are. Anyway, since I knew nothing, I've spent a lot of time reading the old stories, and there are several tales of a wolf claiming their true mate before the human side has caught up, so to speak.”

Arek didn't have time to process this right now. This situation was a fucking mess. “This sounds like something we should discuss later. We need to get out of here.” He needed to get to Laney.

Justice sighed. “That's my whole point. You should be able to connect mentally, or at least emotionally, with Laney if she's your true mate.”

Arek took a long sip of water. He finally felt well enough to stand on his own, without the help of the wall. "What if she's dead?" he finally asked. "What if I connect with her, only to find out Iakov has killed her? My wolf will freak out, and that's not a good thing in these close quarters." He gestured around the small cell. "I may end up killing you both." When a wolf's true mate died, the beast could go insane with grief.

But it wasn't just that.

Arek couldn't face Laney's death. He might not be ready for a relationship with her, but he needed her to be in the world. Even if she was with another man—nope, that was not something he wanted to think about. Too distracting. She couldn't be in the world with another man. She would have to be single if she wasn't with him.

The wolf growled its disagreement. Mine.

"We may have to take that chance," Justice said. "I don't think your wolf will kill pack mates, no matter how rogue he goes. Through the true mate bond, you might be able to ask Laney for help."

"How?" Arek said. "We have no fucking idea where we are." He turned to Bolt. "You're awfully quiet. What do you think?"

"I don't know," his second-in-command answered. "Can't you connect with other pack members instead? Maybe that will be safer."

Arek shook his head. "I can't communicate through the pack bond." He hesitated. How much did he want his wolves to know? They knew he could connect with them, but they may think it intrusive that he could tap into their emotions. "It's a one-way channel," he finally settled on. "I can feel your distress, but I can't send you a message."

"That's my whole point." Justice paced the small space. "An alpha that's bonded with a true mate is supposed to be able to communicate with her."

"You seem to have studied the mating bond in great detail," Bolt said, his eyebrows raised.

"Most of the books in the Pack House library are about wolves finding their mates." Justice shrugged. "I just read what was available. I guess everyone wants a happily ever after."

Arek considered Justice's suggestion. He didn't know how to handle being mated right now, but if he could, he wanted to find out if Laney was all right. He closed his eyes and reached for the bond he had with the pack. Without the medallion, he wouldn't be able to connect with any of the other alphas in the coalition, but he should be able to tap into the connections that he had with the wolves who claimed him as alpha. He reached outward with his senses.

Justice and Bolt had a strong presence in his mind, which made sense, since they were physically close to him. He could feel their distress and frustration, feelings mirroring his own.

He extended the reach of the connection, searching for other pack members and Laney, but nothing but vast emptiness met him. Where before he'd been able to see a web of links with the rest of the pack, there was now nothing.

Frowning, he opened his eyes and stared at Justice. "I sense nothing. It's as if someone's cut off all contact between the rest of the pack and me." He gestured toward the two of them. "Except you two."

Bolt looked around the room. "Maybe they shielded this thing. Like a Faraday cage, but it blocks your alpha connection instead of E&M waves."

Arek had no idea what Bolt talked about, but the shielding part sounded right. It felt like something blocked his pack bonds. He hadn't noticed it before, but now that he consciously thought about it, something inside him was missing.

"Well, that was a dead-end," Justice said. "What do we try next?"

Before Bolt or Arek had a chance to answer, one of the concrete walls dissolved into a shimmering membrane. On the other side, a tall shape of a woman walked toward them, her features coming into focus as she got closer.

Inessa Novikov wrinkled her nose as she watched them through the transparent surface. "Of course, you'd be naked. How distasteful." She waved her hand in the air, and the three of them now wore jeans and white T-shirts.

"Now," she said, looking straight at Arek. "My brother was supposed to be here ages ago. What the fuck have you done with Iakov?

Justice took a step closer to the shimmering wall. "Let us out, and we can discuss it."

Without breaking eye contact with Arek, Inessa twirled her index finger around.

Justice grabbed his throat, making horrible choking sounds.

"I wasn't talking to you, wolfling," the witch said. "I'm conversing with your alpha."

Arek grabbed Justice to keep him from crashing to the floor. His enforcer's face turned blue. "Release him," he shouted. "If you stop choking him, I'll tell you what happened to your brother."

Inessa quirked an eyebrow, but shrugged, and then twirled her finger in the opposite direction.

Justice gasped for air, his wolf growling loudly.

Inessa laughed. "If I wasn't pressed for time to find Iakov, I'd play with you some more, wolfling."

Bolt took a step toward her, and she snapped her head around. "You," she said, her eyebrows raised. "You taste different." She leaned closer. Her eyes focused on Bolt. "Oh, after I find my brother, I want to spend a lot of time with you." She sniffed the air, almost like a wolf. "What are you?" Her eyes widened. "You are delicious."

Bolt shuddered. Arek didn't blame him.

The woman looked deranged.

When she focused back on him, he had to steel himself from taking a step back. "Where is my brother?" the witch demanded.

Fuck. He'd had to make the lie close enough to the truth, or the dark witch would notice the deception.

CHAPTER 19

Drops of water hitting the ground made Laney open her eyes, only to be met with the gruesome sight of Iakov's head floating in the air. The drops she'd heard hitting the ground were the blood leaving his severed neck and splattering on the grass. She rolled the other way and threw up in the grass.

"Oh, shit," a woman said. "I'm sorry. I didn't mean for you to get sick. I just wanted to show you he can't hurt you anymore."

Laney wiped her mouth with the back of her hand and turned toward the voice.

Nora squatted down and placed the dripping head on the ground. She'd been holding it by its hair. In her other hand, a curved blade glinted in the weak rays of dawn. It looked like a machete, and from the deep red liquid coating the steel, it was the tool she had used to behead the mage.

Laney pushed herself off the ground and to her knees. She swayed and plopped her butt on her heels for better balance. Nora reached out to grab her, but she shied away. "I'm fine," Laney said. Nora's hand was coated in grime that she didn't want to see close up or have it touch her skin.

"Shit. Sorry, again." Nora kneeled next to Laney and wiped her hand on first the grass and then her pants.

Laney looked down at her own clothes. The beautiful dress looked like someone had dragged it across a cow pasture. A long rip down the side showed her leg from ankle to mid-thigh. "What happened?"

"That's what I was going to ask you."

Laney studied the woman, eyebrows raised. Nora had held a severed head in one hand and a bloody machete in the other, but she needed Laney to explain what had happened? She shook her head. "The last thing I remember—." Shit, Arek. What had happened to Arek? She looked past Nora, but the only thing visible in the gray light was Iakov's headless body and a pile of clothes. "Where's Arek?" she asked.

"Again," Nora said. "I was hoping you could tell me."

"Arek sensed Bolt being upset, or something." Laney rubbed her face and then wished she hadn't when she saw how muddy her hands were. "We got to this clearing but couldn't find Bolt, only Iakov. He blasted Arek with magic, and then Arek shifted." She frowned. "I opened myself as a conduit to the ley line and hit Iakov with everything I had. That's the last thing I remember."

Nora looked over at the body lying in the grass. "Well, you got him."

"No," Laney protested. She gestured toward the head on the ground. Thankfully, the eyes were closed, but the bleeding neck and the pasty skin made her want to throw up again. She swallowed down the bile. "I didn't do that."

"I know." Nora wiped the large blade on her pant leg and then slipped it behind her back between her shoulder blades and let go of the handle. "I cut off his head."

She stood and walked over to the body. Laney could see that she wore a sheet strapped to her back. The handle of the machete peeked out from the leather. "How?" she asked.

"Hm?" Nora turned toward her. "Oh, with my blade," she said.

Laney pushed herself off the ground and felt proud when she managed to get to her feet with minimal swaying. "No," she searched for the words she wanted. "How did you know where we were, and how did you get close enough to behead Iakov?"

"The second part is easy to answer," Nora said. "I got to the clearing and saw you and Iakov both out cold on the grass. You were both breathing, which in your case was a good thing." She gestured toward the headless body. "In his case, not so much. So, I cut his head off."

Laney blinked at her.

"Look," Nora bristled. "According to pack laws, he intruded on our territory and hurt one of our pack members. I'm totally within my rights to execute him."

"Who?" Laney asked.

"Who what?"

"Which pack member did he hurt?"

Nora's eyebrows shot to her hairline. "You. He hurt you."

"I'm not a pack member," Laney said. This conversation had gone off the rails from the very beginning, and she desperately needed it to get back on track. They needed to find Arek. They should probably get the hell away from the clearing before Inessa decided to look for her brother.

"The alpha's wolf has claimed you. Of course, you're a pack member."

"Who? What, now?" Just when she thought things couldn't get any weirder.

"You're sleeping with Arek, and it's obvious that his wolf has claimed you." Nora picked up the head by the hair again. "We should get out of here, but I'm taking this with me so we can show Nick Novikov what happens when he sends mages to our land."

"Couldn't you just take a picture?"

"Already did," Nora said. "And I'll email that to the other coalitions' commanding alphas. To Novikov, I'll mail this head in a box. I think that will make more of a statement."

"Okay," Laney said, her mind racing as she tried to keep up with the conversation. "Can we get back to the wolf having claims on me?"

Nora walked over to the pile of clothes and picked up the beautiful tuxedo jacket that Arek had worn at the beginning of the evening. As she wrapped it around Iakov's head, Laney shuddered. That fancy garment was now ruined forever.

"Well," the other woman said. "We should probably get out of here and try to find Arek and his lieutenants. Chances are that they hunted down Inessa." She paused and turned back to look at Laney, frowning. "Although that doesn't make any sense. Arek wouldn't have just left you here with Iakov still breathing."

"He shifted," Laney said. "Iakov's magic knocked him down, and he shifted. Maybe he ran off in wolf form?" She desperately hoped that Arek had run off rather than that something horrible had happened to him.

Nora shook her head. "No, even in wolf form, he'd never leave you." She pointed toward the other end of the clearing. "Come on. I have a car parked close to here. We'll regroup there and figure out what to do. Plus, you look like you need some water and food." She started walking.

Something glimmered in the grass next to the clothes. Laney walked over and crouched down to see better. A familiar platinum medallion with a wolf head shaped by runes twinkled on the ground. She picked up Arek's necklace. The chain was intact. It must have slipped off his head when he shifted.

"What did you find?" Nora asked.

Laney held up the medallion. As she did, the beam of sunlight hit the platinum and reflected straight into her eyes. She looked away and gripped the piece harder so she wouldn't drop it. A current of electricity shot up her arm, and she cried out in surprise.

Her eyes teared up, and she had to close them.

Suddenly, she saw Arek in her mind's eye.

He stood next to Justin and Bolt. They argued with a woman, but her features were out of focus as if Laney viewed her through water.

Arek's head shot up, and he turned around. "Laney?" he whispered in her mind.

The medallion grew glowing hot, and she dropped it. A blinding headache assaulted her, and she gasped, falling to her knees.

Nora rushed to her side. "Are you okay? Do you need me to carry you?" She cupped her elbow and helped Laney back up.

"I'm fine." Laney cleared her throat. "I saw Arek and the other two."

"Where?" Nora's voice grew urgent. "Did you recognize their location?"

Laney shook her head. "They were in a small room with a weird wall. They argued with a woman."

"Inessa?"

"Could be, but I can't say for sure." She reached down and picked up the medallion by its chain. "I want to try again to see if I can get a location this time."

Nora frowned. "Are you sure? It looked like the piece hurt you."

Laney nodded. "Very sure." If she could forge a connection with Arek, maybe he could tell them where he was. She steeled herself against the pain and gripped the Odin artifact again.

Holding it between her palms, she waited for the heat to sear her skin. But this time, instead of giving her a blast of fiery agony, the jewelry warmed up gradually.

Laney closed her eyes, concentrating on the connection she'd felt with Arek before. No image came to her, but her hands shook, twitching. The medallion seemed attached to an invisible force that pulled her along in its wake.

She took a few steps, and the force got stronger, forcing her to jog across the clearing. She opened her eyes so she wouldn't stumble on the uneven ground.

"Hang on," Nora shouted. "That's the wrong direction from the car."

Laney tried to stop, but the invisible force pulled on her hands, and the medallion's temperature increased. When she was close to running full out, she let go of the jewelry.

The platinum medal dropped to the grass and flashed icy white.

Nora caught up with her. "I think we should get in the car and test out this weird magical GPS. We don't know how far away they are, provided this thing guides us to Arek's location. I can run for miles in wolf form, but you don't even have shoes on." She grinned.

Laney looked down at her bare feet. They were as grimy as the rest of her. "Do you have any spare clothes in the car?"

"Of course." Nora winked. "All self-respecting shifters carry at least one change of clothes. Let's get you geared up and clothed." She picked up Iakov's head and strode through the grass. "And then we'll get the dark witch's head. I'm looking forward to sending Novikov a matching pair."

They reached the car, an SUV with tinted back windows and a huge cargo hold. Nora opened the back and retrieved a pack of baby wipes. She took a few out and handed the pack to Laney. "I know it's weird," the tall woman said. "But sometimes I just don't want to get in the car all gory after I've hunted in wolf form or got muddy during a run." She rummaged around some more in the back of the car and pulled out an empty cardboard box in which she deposited the tuxedo-jacket-wrapped head.

Laney used the wipes to clean off as much of the mud covering her body as she could. Nora handed her a pair of black yoga pants and a pink long-sleeved t-shirt that on the back said, "Wolves Do It with a Growl." When Laney quirked an eyebrow, the lawyer just shrugged. "It was free," she said, handing over a pair of socks and trainers. "I think we have the same size."

The shoes fit perfectly. "Anything else useful in there?" Laney asked, peeking into the back of the car.

Nora grinned and opened the door wider.

Sunlight glinted off row after row of specially mounted racks filled with blades of every size imagined.

"Wow," Laney said. "You really like knives."

"I do. I really do." Nora sighed happily. "I can't wait to test out some of these on Inessa."

CHAPTER 20

Dizziness made Arek take a sidestep and stumble. He could have sworn Laney had been here with him.

He'd smelled her.

Mate, his wolf growled. *Where's Mate?*

So, it wasn't just Arek. His beast had noticed Laney's presence too. What the fuck was going on?

Bolt and Justice shot him curious looks. "Are you okay?" Bolt mouthed silently.

Arek nodded and mentally shook himself. He looked back at Inessa.

The dark witch had features that should make her beautiful, but her lips seemed permanently pursed in displeasure, and her eyes glittered with cruelty. The ugliness of her personality and power shone through her flawless skin. "Stop playing games, alpha. Where is my brother?"

"He's still at Villa Montalvo," Arek said. "At least he was when I left." He cleared his throat and instantly regretted it. His throat was dry, but maybe Inessa would see it as a sign of lying. Which it wasn't, technically.

Fuck. Had he hallucinated, Laney?

Did she die, and the true mate bond—if Justice was right—had somehow messed with his head?

Bolt nudged him, and Arek turned to face him. His lieutenant gestured toward Inessa.

Oh shit, the witch had been talking, and he'd missed whatever she'd said.

"Some persuasion seems to be needed." The witch twisted her hand.

In an instant, Justice disappeared from the cell and reappeared on the other side of the barrier, next to Inessa.

Arek clenched his jaw so hard he thought he'd crack a tooth.

"Shit," Bolt said and rammed the wall with his shoulder. It remained solid.

He launched himself against it again.

Same result.

On the other side, Justin stood frozen next to the dark witch. His eyes moved as he glared at Inessa, but the rest of his body appeared like a statue.

The witch slowly walked around him, her fingernail trailing from one shoulder, across his chest, to the other shoulder, and then across his back.

She leaned in and sniffed him just above his collarbone. "Mm, tasty." She raised her head and locked eyes with Bolt. "Not as delicious as you, my friend, but all shifters have magic inside them. I'm looking forward to unlocking this one's."

Arek tried to think of something to say that would stop her from doing whatever horrible thing she was about to start.

Justice stared defiantly at the witch. A tic in his jaw twitched as she gripped the hem of his t-shirt and slowly lifted it to reveal his abdominal muscles and chest.

Bolt cursed and took a step back. He kicked the wall over and over again, but it didn't budge.

Inessa pulled Justice's shirt over his head. The lieutenant's neck muscles strained, but he still didn't move.

She placed her finger over his lips. "Shh, little wolfling. This won't hurt for very long." She giggled. "It will be pain such that you have never experienced before. But I'll keep the first burst short."

Arek joined Bolt in trying to kick down the wall, but with their bare feet, all they managed to do was hurt themselves.

The witch turned around and stared at Arek. "Watch, alpha. See what happens to those you swore to protect when you don't do as I ask." She twisted her fingers in front of Justice's mouth, as if turning a key, and then stepped back so Bolt and Arek could see his face.

Smooth, solid skin covered his lower face without a single dip or crease.

The witch had removed his mouth and nose.

Justice's eyes bulged, and his body twitched. He was suffocating.

Ice icy rage filled Arek's veins. He reached for his wolf to shift, but couldn't bring the beast to the surface. His body buckled and twisted but wouldn't reshape into the wolf. Inside him, his beast howled.

Bolt watched him with horrified eyes. "I can't shift," he said. "She's stolen my wolf."

Inessa watched them both from the other side with cold eyes. "Aw, poor wolfies. Did I forget to say that you can't shift in that cell?"

Fucking dark witch. Arek would tear her limb from limb as soon as he got out of this dammed concrete box.

In horror, he watched Justice's eyes roll into the back of his head.

Inessa's eyes glittered as she observed Arek and Bolt watching Justice's suffering.

Justice would die because of him, because he didn't protect his pack from this dark witch. Because he wasn't alpha enough to stop Inessa and Iakov from entering his territory. What useless alpha didn't protect his pack territory?

Bolt slapped him. "What the fuck is wrong with you? We don't have time for your pity party. She's killing Justice."

Had he said all those things out loud? His eyes narrowed as he looked at the witch.

The self-satisfied smirk on her face convinced him she'd been messing with his head. "What kind of pathetic dark witch are you?" Anger made his voice hoarse. "I thought the bargain for giving up your soul was to become all-powerful."

Inessa frowned. "What are you babbling about, alpha?" Behind her, Justice collapsed to the floor, but she didn't turn around. Her remained gaze focused on Arek.

"Why can't you locate your brother yourself?" he shouted. "If you are both dark magic wielders, shouldn't you be able to find out where he is?"

"I've searched all of Villa Montalvo and the gardens," Inessa said. "I could find him anywhere, but it will take too long to search all possible locations." She looked away. Something wasn't right about that statement, but

Arek didn't have time to play games. Justice's body convulsed on the floor. He didn't have long.

"Release my lieutenant, and I'll give you a clue about where your brother is, since you don't seem capable of finding him on your own." He smirked. "Or does he not want to be found? Maybe he's not as fond of you as you think."

The witch waited for a beat and then twitched her hand. Justice's mouth and nose returned. He drew in a long gasp of breath and then turned to retch water on the floor.

Beside Arek, Bolt exhaled his relief.

"Hurry up, wolf," Inessa said. "My brother is as devoted to me as I am to him. Something must have happened to him to detain him for this long. I'm sure he amused himself with your little earthbound witch, but he'd be done with her by now."

"He's in the El Sereno Preserve greenbelt," Arek said, refusing to rise to her bait. "That's where he was before you pulled me here."

The witch frowned. "Why would he go into the forest? If he wanted the earthbound witch, that's the worst place to hunt her. Her magic—." She cut herself off and studied Arek. "Where is this greenbelt in relation to the villa?"

Arek thought about misleading her, but decided not to take the risk. "Straight south," he said.

A knife appeared in the witch's hand. She knelt by Justice, who flinched but seemed unable to move more than that.

The blade flashed as Inessa swung it down, cutting the side of Justice's neck.

Bolt roared out his anger at the same time as Arek shouted, "No."

The witch rolled her eyes at them and snapped her fingers.

Justice appeared back in the cell. Arek pulled off his shirt and applied it to Justice's neck to stanch the flow of blood.

His enforcer whispered, "That witch is so far beyond wicked. She's straight-up evil."

"Don't talk," Arek said, pressing against the wound. He took a deep breath as the blood flow finally slowed and eventually stopped. The cut hadn't been deep.

Meanwhile, the dark witch kneeled with the bloody blade held between her palms. She raised her arms so that the knife tip was above her head and tilted her head back. Blood slowly dripped from the metal down into her mouth.

Bolt gagged.

Arek didn't blame him. He didn't mind the taste of raw blood during the full moon hunt. But the witch was a little too happy to drink Justice's blood. She hummed and swayed as the red drops flowed into her mouth.

Fucking gross.

Her head snapped forward, and her eyes rolled into the back of her head so that only the whites showed.

"Fucking evil, I say," Justice whispered.

"Fucking witches. I hate them," Bolt muttered.

Laney was nothing like this deranged woman, and Arek was about to tell him that when an inhuman wail assaulted his eardrums.

The witch's eyes snapped back, fury blazing out of them as she locked gazes with Arek. "You killed him," she shrieked. "You and your fucking witch beheaded him and left his body to rot in the forest."

Fuck.

Whatever deranged vision she had seen, it meant terrible news for him and his wolves.

"Incoming," Justice shouted as Inessa rose and launched herself at them, the bloody knife held high, dripping onto her dress.

The transparent wall that had been indestructible when Arek and Bolt had tried to get to Justice shimmered one last time and disappeared.

The three wolves immediately stepped outside the cement prison cell, ripped off their clothes, and shifted.

If the barrier between them and the deranged dark witch was down, facing her as wolves was the better option.

Perhaps the only option, if they were to survive.

CHAPTER 21

Nora drove the way she beheaded people, sharply and decisively, and with a lot of mess left in the wake.

"You just ran that stop sign," Laney said, looking behind them. The horns of the other cars grew distant as Nora sped them away from the intersection.

"Don't worry about how I drive," the lawyer said. "Concentrate on where I'm supposed to go."

Laney thought about pointing out the contradiction in that statement, but instead closed her eyes and focused on the tugs and pulls that showed which way the medallion wanted them to go.

She held the artifact cupped in her palms. That way, the heat of the metal didn't bother her as much as when she squeezed it between her hands. The jewelry glowed and gave off a blaze of heat that increased the further they drove.

"Turn left," she told Nora without opening her eyes, but winced when she heard the squealing of rubber against asphalt.

From how the car leaned, she could tell Nora took the corner on two wheels. And from the angry honking, she cut off a few cars to take the turn.

They had been driving south on highway nine, but were now going west on highway seventeen, heading into the Santa Cruz Mountain foothills, toward the Lexington Reservoir.

The medallion's temperature increased, and Laney had to take deep breaths as it burnt her skin again.

"You okay?" Nora asked, squeezing her knee. When the other woman touched her, the metal of the jewelry cooled while the pull on Laney's hand became stronger.

"Keep doing that," she said.

"Keep doing what?"

"Touching me. I don't know why, but it focuses the medallion."

Nora did as asked, and now Laney could see images in her mind. "They're in a garage or something that's used to store vehicles." She frowned. "I can't get a clear picture of the outside, but the inside is mostly concrete." She paused, focusing on the images broadcasting in her mind.

"And it's close to water. On the shore of a large body of water."

"Could it be a fire station?" Nora asked. "The forestry service has a station right on the edge of the reservoir."

"Yes," Laney said when Nora's words clarified the images in her head. "There are several buildings and a helicopter pad."

"I know exactly where that is." The lawyer pushed down the gas pedal, and the SUV shot forward.

Laney dropped the medallion and grabbed the door handle to stay in her seat. She gasped as Nora crashed through a pair of metal-framed chicken wire gates without slowing down and continued down a driveway. They sped through a deserted parking lot.

"This station is in use," the lawyer said. "There should be people and cars here at all hours."

"Inessa could have used dark magic to convince them all to go home," Laney said. The car had finally slowed down enough to where she could reach for the medallion on the floor. As soon as she grabbed it, she got a flash of Arek. He'd shifted to wolf. "There," she pointed to a building with big bay doors. "That's where they are."

Nora punched the gas pedal again and drove straight through the bay doors. They crumpled with horrible noises of grinding metal and shattering glass.

The SUV skidded sideways before the lawyer got it under control. She stood on the break.

The squeal of tires against concrete reached Laney's ears at the same time as the stench of burning rubber invaded her nose.

She paid it no attention, though, because her eyes were on the drama unfolding in front of her, inside the station.

Three wolves faced off against Inessa. They hunched low, their lips pulled back in snarls, as they advanced on the dark witch.

Laney recognized Arek's gray wolf and Bolt's silver. The gray and brown brindle had to be Justice.

Nora jumped out of the car, slamming the door behind her. "Hello, boys. Did you miss me?" She pulled the machete from the sheet strapped to her back. "I want the witch's head. It matches the one I have in the back of the car."

Inessa shrieked and turned away from the wolves, advancing toward Nora instead. "You killed my brother."

"I did," Nora said, holding her blade with both hands in front of her. She widened her stance and rotated her shoulders. "What are you going to do about it?"

Laney wanted to tell her to stop taunting the dark witch. Inessa didn't need proximity to strike, but then she saw that the wolves had advanced behind the dark witch while Nora had distracted her. The lawyer had drawn the witch's attention on purpose.

Laney jumped out of the car and slipped the medallion around her neck. She didn't know why, but it had been her guiding talisman, and so she'd rather have it with her than leave it in the car.

The silver wolf rushed the witch and jumped. His fangs sunk deep into her neck, and he snarled as he tore at her skin.

Inessa clapped her hands together, and an invisible wind blew the wolf away from her, slamming him into the wall.

He whimpered as he slid down on the floor, one of the hind legs at an awkward angle.

Laney closed her eyes and reached out with her senses, looking for a ley line. She wasn't sure she could pull on the magic after opening herself wide as a conduit when she blasted Iakov. She might have fried her systems.

Relief flooded her mind when she felt the familiar pull of potent magic. A current of power ran down the middle of the reservoir. The combination of running water above a ley line made it easier to tap into the power, and she drew from the clean earthbound energy, feeling rejuvenated she'd never experienced.

Suddenly, the dark witch turned her way and focused her cruel, cold eyes on Laney. "Oh no, you don't get to pull on your feeble earthbound power," she hissed. "It's your fault my brother is dead. If he hadn't chased after you, we'd have slaughtered and skinned the alpha and his two lieutenants by now." She took a step toward Laney. "And I'd be sketching designs of a fur coat for my tailor."

Arek's wolf snarled and placed himself in front of Laney, a growling, pawing barrier of muscle and fur between her and the dark witch. In wolf form, Arek was the size of a small pony.

"Hello," Nora called. "I'm the one who cut your brother's ugly head." She held out the machete. "Want to touch the blade that severed his neck?"

Inessa kept her gaze locked with Laney's but flicked her hand toward the lawyer. A blast of power punched Nora backward and into the grill of the SUV. She cried out and crumpled to the floor.

The brindle wolf ran over to her and nudged her with his nose. He whimpered when Nora didn't move.

Inessa kept advancing on Laney, who gathered her power around her. She knew she couldn't open herself up as a conduit again, not if she wanted to survive. Filling her inside well with magic was already more effort than usual. She swayed on her feet and grabbed onto Arek for support.

As her hand touched his pelt, the medallion around her neck blazed blinding white. The overhead lights popped one-by-one. Glass rained down as sparks of electricity sizzled in the air.

A strength Laney had never felt before flowed through her body, filling her reserves to the brim, and still, she could pull in more without overloading her senses.

The gray wolf turned to look at her with icy-blue eyes. *Do you feel this?* Arek's voice asked in her head.

Yes, she answered through the connection which he had spoken and pulled in even more power.

Inessa raised her hands, sparks of magic arching between her palms to form a glowing ball of power. Her lips moved, but Laney couldn't make out what spell the dark witch chanted. She probably wouldn't recognize it if she could.

The ball grew in size, and Laney pushed everything she had into a magical shield she erected to protect herself and Arek from Inessa's incoming assault. The wolf crouched down as if preparing to leap.

Don't, Laney commanded through their connection. *I can't hold the shield if you jump through it.*

The wolf growled and pawed at the ground, but some of the tension left its body.

Inessa palmed the ball in one hand and raised it higher.

She threw the glowing globe of power toward Laney, who pushed every ounce of magic she could into the protective shield.

A loud bang reverberated through the building and a blaze of green light blinded Laney. She closed her eyes against the intensity of the flare.

When she opened them again, Inessa had vanished, and a stench of burning hair lingered in the air.

The gray wolf wrinkled its nose and sneezed. *Are you okay?* Arek's voice asked in her head.

She nodded.

On the other side of the garage, a naked Bolt sat up. He groaned as he held his head. "Fucking witch ran away scared."

Justice had also shifted and kneeled next to Nora. "Her breathing is steady," he called out. "She's going to have one hell of a concussion, but I think she's going to be okay."

Laney looked around the room. The bay doors were completely demolished. Shattered glass covered every surface, and several of the lights hung from the ceiling by only a wire or two.

The firefighters and forestry personnel were in for a surprise when they came to work in the morning.

EPILOGUE

The afternoon sun warmed his skin as Arek walked across the lawn to the back terrace where Laney sat with one of his old ledgers.

The last few days had been busy. They'd cleared out of the fire station without getting noticed. The local paper had reported that a freak tornado must have touched down on the edge of Lexington Reservoir but destroyed only one building, leaving the others intact.

Arek had arranged for a large anonymous donation that should take care of the damage and still leave enough for a new fire engine or two.

Bolt's leg had healed perfectly the next time he shifted into his wolf. Nora's concussion hadn't been as easy to fix, but with rest, she should also completely recover. She wouldn't stop talking about mailing Iakov's head to the Novikovs. Unfortunately, that would probably never happen.

He frowned, thinking of the conference video call he'd just completed with the alphas of the Western Pack Coalition. Arek had been all for shipping the gruesome package to Nick and Inessa, but the council requested a less overt gesture of aggression. Too much diplomacy was on the line. Once Nora recovered from the concussion, her lawyer brain would tell her so.

However, by the end of the meeting, there'd been no clear decision of what action to take. The alphas wanted more discussion. Arek didn't see why. The Novikovs had trespassed in his territory. They needed to be dealt with swiftly, or they'd keep violating the Pack Directives.

But that was a worry for another day. He'd rarely seen Laney during these few days, and the two hadn't had a chance to talk. Something he wanted to rectify right away.

He climbed the two steps up to the patio and approached the table where she sat. "Mind if I join you?"

She looked up, shielding her eyes against the sun with one hand. "No," she said, smiling, but it was tentative.

He knew how she felt. Speaking mind-to-mind had been freaky. He'd tried to repeat it but hadn't been successful. It probably only worked when they had physical contact while he was in wolf form.

Arek pulled out a chair and sat. He cleared his throat. "How's the cataloging going?"

"I'm making progress." She pushed her hair away from her face. "But it's going to take a long time to get it all organized."

"Does that mean you'll stay for a while?" He liked the idea of her staying in the house for a long time.

She hesitated. "You mean, live here? Or do you mean work here?"

He tried to read her face to see which option she preferred, but he couldn't tell. Her amber eyes calmly met his, although, from the pulse in her neck beating rapidly, he knew she wasn't as serene as she pretended to be.

Still, it didn't give him a clue as to which choice she'd rather make. *Note to self. Don't play poker with this witch.* "Whatever you are comfortable with," he finally said, grabbing her hand and pulling it toward him.

No, his wolf growled. *Mate lives here.*

Laney jumped. "Was that what...who I think it was?"

Arek nodded, watching her carefully for any signs of fear. "Yeah, he likes to butt in at the most inconvenient times."

She tilted her head. "I could hear him in my mind, just like we talked to each other at the fire station."

"Does it scare you when he does that?"

"Which time?"

"Either." He held his breath, waiting for her answer. There was no doubt that they were true mates, but he didn't want to force something on her that she wasn't prepared for.

She paused for a beat. "No," she finally said. "It's interesting. A little weird. But not scary."

"So, this thing with the wolf." He paused.

"Nora says you and I are true mates." Laney pulled her hand back, and he immediately missed the contact.

"She's right." He cleared his throat. "How do you feel about that?"

She searched his face. "How do you feel about that?"

He smiled. Answering a question with a question was his favorite evasive move. "I honestly don't know." He grabbed her hand again. "It's sudden and strange. But yet, it somehow feels right."

"Yeah," she whispered, and then cleared her throat. "Nora also said that wolves mate for life and go insane if their true mate dies or abandons them."

"Nora has explained a lot about the mating of wolves."

"I kind of asked her about it." Laney smiled. "According to her, I interrogated her."

He reached for her other hand, holding both in his. "I don't want you to feel pressured into anything." He wanted her to stay, but not if it wasn't her choice.

"What do you want?" she asked. "Tell me how you see this working?"

He laughed. "I have no freaking idea. But I know I want you here, with me, while we figure out how this can work for both of us."

Her smile lit up his heart. "I like that," she said. "I like that very much."

Mate stays, the wolf purred.

Laney giggled.

Stupid beast. Always had to have the last word.

Arek leaned over the table and claimed his mate's lips.

For once, the wolf remained quiet.

WANT to know how Nora meets her true mate? Read on for a sneak preview of *Berserker Devotion* and check out the rest of the books in the *Norse Warrior Protectors*: https://www.asamariabradley.com/norsewarriorprotectors/.

Thank you for reading my stories!

BERSERKER DEVOTION PREVIEW

Chapter 1

Despite the four-wheel-drive mode, the rented SUV's wheels slipped in the deep snow that covered the forest road. Ulf Stenrik swore as the vehicle lost traction and slid off the road. The car had probably hit a ditch because the SUV tilted at an angle with the hood lower than the rest of the vehicle. He'd been lucky to make it this far without getting stuck in a trench. The landscape was completely covered in deep snow. Determining where the road ended and the ditch began had been impossible.

At least he knew where that transition was now.

He pulled on his knit cap, zipped up the down jacket, and slipped on gloves. Leaving the engine running and the gear in neutral, Ulf opened the door and scrambled out. He landed in knee-deep snow that immediately slid inside his boots.

And that was before he had to step into the ditch.

Cursing again, he steeled himself against more coldness and wetness filling his footwear as he waded into the deeper snow until he'd reached the front of the car.

The blanketed landscape muffled all sound, and the only thing he could hear was the rumble of the engine. Not even the birds chirped. The effect would have been spooky if it wasn't for the bright overhead sun reflecting off every snow-covered pine tree and the road itself. The glittering mess hurt his eyes despite the dark sunglasses he wore. Squinting, he crouched down and gripped the frame below the front bumper of the SUV.

Even for an immortal Viking like him, lifting the vehicle's engine block—which probably weighed about five hundred pounds or so—took a lot of effort. Sweating and grunting, he managed to maneuver the car back onto the road, but it was obvious that even there, the snow was too deep to continue driving.

"*Jävlar, helvetes, skit,*" he swore out loud in Swedish.

A bird thrilled in response to his outburst, and soon a choir of feathered creatures joined in.

Apparently, nature had decided to wake up, and on any other day at any other place, the sunshine, the snow-sparkling forest, and the cheerful birdsong would have cheered up Ulf. Here and now, it just felt like the fucking birds were laughing at him. Like they'd kept quiet while they'd watched him struggle with the car and now found his predicament hilarious.

He was stuck deep in a national forest in the California Sierra Mountains in December.

And his feet were cold. And wet.

The worst part was that he'd volunteered for this stupid trip. King Leif wanted a particular bear sculpture from a particular woodcarver, and since Ulf still needed to build up some goodwill among his immortal Norse battle brothers and sisters, he'd volunteered. He wasn't exactly in the dog house anymore, but his stint as an arrogant jackass for several months had not been forgotten. He still needed to rebuild a lot of trust.

He looked down what he assumed was the road. Its pristine snow cover mocked him in its glittering beauty.

The fucking woodcarver lived in a remote cabin way further up the mountain. Why couldn't he sell his sculptures on the internet like most people? The guy didn't even have a website. The king had read about him in some obscure magazine. Ulf turned off the car's engine. No reason to keep it on since he was obviously not driving any further.

His cellphone chimed and vibrated in his pocket. When he dug it out, he saw the king's name on the screen and swallowed a sigh before clicking the button to receive the call.

"Are you there yet?" Leif asked without a greeting.

"No, I'm still about fifteen kilometers away."

The king sighed loudly. "What's taking you so long?

Considering Ulf had flown from Washington State to Nevada, picked up the rental SUV, and then driven across the state line into California and the eastern part of the Sierra Mountains, he'd actually made pretty good time. However, the king was not known for having a lot of patience—and lately, his sense of humor had been non-existent—so Ulf refrained from explaining how travel worked. "I've hit a bit of a snag," he said instead.

"What?" Leif exclaimed loudly.

Ulf's berserker, his inner warrior spirit, perked up, responding to the urgency in the king's voice. Ulf mentally commanded it to stand down. "Don't worry," he said quickly. "Everything is under control. It's just that the road has too much snow for the car to drive through."

"Well, put it in four-wheel-drive." The king's voice was still over-the-top loud. But the poor guy had been overreacting to pretty much everything ever since he'd found out his *själsfrände*, his true love, was pregnant. There hadn't been a child born to an immortal Viking before. The bond between the king and his human mate was unusual, although Queen Naya was no ordinary human. She'd been genetically engineered into an ultimate soldier.

"*Min Kung*," Ulf said in as calm of a voice he could manage, "the SUV has been in four-wheel drive for several miles. But the snow is knee-deep and wet and heavy. I would need a sled or a snowmobile to get through this."

"Well, get one of those then. The Norse bear carving is the perfect *Julgåva* for Naya. She has her heart set on it."

Ulf could barely keep his sigh contained. Naya probably didn't even know she was getting a wooden bear for Christmas. He doubted the queen even liked woodcarvings, but the king had been obsessed with the thing ever since he saw the magazine article. "Driving back down the mountain to the closest town will take too long." He refrained from mentioning that the word "town" was a bit generous for the small cluster of houses nestled against the foot of the mountain. There had been no rental shop or any kind of commercial building that he'd seen. The most he could probably hope for was to knock on someone's house and ask for some snowshoes or skis. "I'll lose the daylight if I go back, and I doubt I'll have enough cell signal to be able to navigate to the guy's cabin in the dark."

The king muttered something. It sounded like it was about youngsters being lazy and weak. Considering that the king was only three years older when he died and went to Valhalla than Ulf was when he passed away on the battlefield and took his seat in Odin's afterlife beer-hall, it was a bit much for the king to call him a youngster. But then again, Odin sent Leif back to Midgard forty years before Ulf had joined the band of immortal Norse warriors in the human realm, so maybe that was why the king considered himself more mature.

Ulf ignored the king's words and instead assured him that he would continue on foot and be back at the tribe's mansion in a few days with the carved bear.

The king muttered a bit more but seemed placated by Ulf's assurances, and they hung up.

Now, if only he could somehow assure himself that he'd make it to this cabin in the middle of nowhere before nightfall. Why had this woodcarver chosen such a remote home? Living "off-the-grid," as modern-time mortals called it, seemed bonkers. Ulf remembered a time when electricity, refrigeration, and indoor plumbing were not yet invented, and he had no desire to recreate how he'd lived back then.

He dug out a pair of dry socks from his bag in the back of the SUV and exchanged them for the wet ones on his feet. He pulled out the granola bars and trail mix he'd brought and stuffed them in his pants and jacket pockets. The cell phone map showed the switchbacks the road took to the cabin, but on foot, he'd be able to travel a more direct route. Since he didn't know for how long he'd have a signal, he dug out a pen and some paper and sketched a rough outline of the map and what seemed like a good route to his destination.

Finally, there was no other reason to prolong the time before he'd have to start trekking. He pulled his cap further down on his head and straightened his sunglasses.

After two steps, his boots were filled with snow again.

"Jävlar, helvetes, skit."

Nobody but the birds heard him, and those little fuckers just kept on singing their happy little tunes. Why did he volunteer to make this bonkers trip without properly researching how remote the cabin was? Now he had no choice but to keep putting one wet and cold foot in front of the other wet and cold foot until he got to the woodcarver's home.

Returning without the wooden bear was not an option.

Ulf had never failed his king before and would not be bested by something as trivial as a Norse wooden bear.

Chapter 2

The man came out of nowhere.

Well, obviously, he came from somewhere, but Nora Bretagne hadn't expected him.

One minute she was running in her wolf form in the forest, listening to the birds' happy trilling while she broke trail in the deep snow.

The next minute, a man stepped out from between the trees and startled her.

If she hadn't been so worried about her uncle, the guy would never have been able to sneak up on her.

If she hadn't been distracted by the birds' loud song, she would have heard him coming.

If she'd been more observant, she could have avoided this confrontation and hid from him until she could follow him to see why he'd ventured this far into the mountains.

On foot.

Without snowshoes or skis.

Did he not know how snow worked?

Dark sunglasses obscured his eyes, so she couldn't gauge what he might do next from looking into them. Instead, she kept her gaze on his hands, waiting for him to reach for a weapon. The fur on the back of her neck stood, and her lips curled back into a snarl. The reaction was as much defensive as it was a response to the frustration she felt for messing up and letting him surprise her.

The guy reared back, stumbled on something buried in the snow, and fell flat on his back. He did not get up again.

Gingerly, she approached his prone form, ready to jump back if he made any sudden moves. She'd been fooled by someone playing dead once before, and she had the scar across her face to remind her why she'd never let that happen again.

The man didn't move.

Not even when she nudged him with her nose. He smelled...different.

She sniffed him again, trying to discern what made his scent unusual. Regular humans lacked the spicy undertones that shifters' fragrance carried. And wolves had a particular scent signature that reminded her of deep woods and mulch. This man smelled of fire and hot metal, like a forge. He definitely wasn't a regular human but also didn't have the earthiness and spice of magic. Which meant he wasn't a witch.

And yet, finding a supernatural being this far into the woods worried her. Did he have something to do with her uncle's disappearance?

She nudged him again and then grabbed the sleeve of his jacket when he didn't react. She shook his arm hard. Her teeth pierced the fabric of the garment, and little puffs of down fluttered out. Still no response from the man, but he breathed evenly. He'd somehow knocked himself out cold.

Nora looked around the glen they were in as if she'd find something or someone to help her. Of course, she found nothing and nobody. Except for the birds, she and the man were alone.

She filled her mouth with snow. The cold against her teeth gave her a brain freeze. She spat it out into the man's face with a little more force than necessary, which knocked off the sunglasses and revealed more of his handsome face.

His breath hitched for a short moment but then resumed its steady inhales and exhales. His eyelids didn't even flutter. For all appearances, the man looked like he'd just lied down for a nice little nap in the middle of a snowdrift.

Since he wasn't all-human, he probably wouldn't freeze to death if she just left him here. However, if he knew where her uncle was or what had happened to him, then she wanted to interrogate him. Somehow, she needed to get him back to her uncle's cabin and secure him, all before he woke up. But they were quite some distance away from that cabin.

It would only take her minutes to run back on her own, but she also needed to get the man back there.

She puffed out a breath of air, which misted in the cold, as she contemplated her options.

In wolf form, she traveled faster through the snow, but there was no way to carry the man. In human form, she'd be able to lift him—wolf shifters were stronger than regular humans—but she'd be naked, which didn't bother her except walking barefoot in snow would be cold and painful.

Nora eyed the man's boots. They were way too big for her feet. If she tried to walk in them, she'd probably slip out of them when the deep snow gripped them. Also, the thought of wearing a stranger's sweaty footwear grossed her out.

She looked at the trail she'd broken from the cabin to this glen and made her choice. She would have to drag him through the snow.

She tried to put the sunglasses back on the man's face, but they refused to cooperate. Precious minutes were wasted while she nudged the frames into their folded position and inside the man's jacket. She loved running as wolf, but there were times when thumbs were very practical.

A thorough sniff-down didn't reveal any weapons in his pockets. She didn't bother trying to open them since she only smelled snacks, no metal of guns or knives.

Her stomach growled. It had been a while since she'd eaten, and when she ran as wolf, she burned more calories than as a human. Maybe she'd relieve the man of some of his granola bars once she got him back to her uncle's cabin. It was the least he owed her for not leaving him passed out in the cold snow.

Gripping the collar of the man's fluffy jacket, she walked backward down the trail she'd broken through the deep snow, dragging the man with her.

The man's weight, combined with the effort of walking backward, made progress slow. Plus, his ridiculously large boots kept catching on twigs and pebbles in the snow. She had to switch her bite several times on the jacket collar because her jaw ached with the effort of moving him and also from her clenching down harder than necessary in frustration.

At one point, the man groaned, and she stopped to see if he would wake up. Although his eyelids fluttered for a moment, he remained unconscious, and so she continued her trek.

More than an hour later, she finally reached the outskirts of the clearing in which the cabin stood. She rested and caught her breath before she dug in again and dragged her load to the steps of her uncle's rustic home. The expensive down jacket looked a mess. Her teeth had caused small feathers to leak from the collar, but twigs and other sharp things on the trail had shredded most of the back of the garment.

Dark clouds had rolled in while she'd dragged the man through the forest, and now fat snowflakes fell from the sky. The trail she's broken would be filled in again.

Shifting into human form, Nora risked leaving the man for the few minutes it took her to enter the cabin and get dressed. She then returned outside and hoisted him up the steps and inside.

All she had to do now was secure her prisoner, wait for him to regain consciousness, and then interrogate him until he told her what had happened to her uncle.

Thank you for reading! Want more? Order *Berserker Devotion* now and check out the rest of the books in the *Norse Warrior Protectors:* https://www.asamariabradley.com/norsewarriorprotectors/.

If you haven't already, subscribe to my newsletter for new releases updates, bonus content, and exclusive giveaways: www.asamariabradley.com/newsletter/

BONUS SHORT STORY WOLF DESIRE

He found her. His wolf claimed her. He'll do anything to save her.

Thirty years ago, wolf shifter and self-made billionaire Magnus Flink challenged and killed his sadistic alpha to stop him from torturing and murdering pack members. He's been a rogue ever since and wants nothing to do with pack politics. But now, a war is brewing between the four major shifter coalitions.

And when a power-hungry alpha wields dark magic to kidnap the woman Magnus's wolf has claimed as mate, he'll have to stretch the limits of his abilities—animal and human—to save her.

CHAPTER 1

Magnus Flink adjusted the collar of his tuxedo shirt and wished he could undo the top button, but that would make his bowtie lopsided. As much as he hated formal dress, the tux was more than just clothing in this environment. It was protection.

The members of Denver's high society, currently mingling in the lobby of the Museum of Art, pretended to be the closest of friends, but any fashion faux pas counted as a chink in one's armor. Magnus never showed weakness.

As a shifter, the wolf inside him wouldn't allow it.

A server passed by with a tray of champagne glasses, and Magnus grabbed one. His metabolism burned alcohol too fast for it to have any effect, but holding a skimpy glass of the piss-colored liquid was better than skulking around with clenched fists as he navigated the tall tables dotted around the marble-floored lobby for yet another charity auction.

Passing three beautiful women, he smiled politely. The blonde in the middle gave him a once over, which he ignored. Instead, he stayed on course toward the back of the room. He was here for one reason only: to chase down the woman his wolf had decided would be their mate.

He found an empty table by a wall, which he leaned against as he surveyed the crowd. Another couple of women, and one of the men, glanced his way appreciatively. He knew people found him attractive, but it wasn't just because of his looks. You could dress up any thug in an expensive tux, and people would faun all over him.

And thinking of ugly thugs, here was one now. The commanding alpha of the Western Packs, Arek Varg, entered the venue, scanned the room, and then set a course straight for Magnus. He sighed inwardly and resisted the urge to escape. Wolf called to wolf. There was no way to hide from a fellow shifter.

Arek plowed through the crowd, his piercing sky-blue eyes even more intense than usual. Dressed in a black button-down shirt tucked into slacks, also black, he looked underdressed.

"Nice outfit," Magnus said when Arek walked up. "Shouldn't an alpha dress better to the occasion?"

The other shifter stepped to the opposite side of the table and put his back against the wall. "I didn't pack a monkey suit because I didn't know I'd have to track you down at a circus." His disdain showed clearly on his face as he looked around the room. "Why aren't you answering calls or texts?"

Magnus shrugged. "I'm busy." He stared at the ancient platinum medallion Arek wore instead of a tie. It was a wolf head inscribed with runes, with three interlocking triangles on its forehead. The triangles symbolized Odin. Like Magnus, the alpha had been born in Scandinavia, but several decades before himself. Rumors said the medallion had magical powers.

Magnus met the alpha's hard gaze—because he could. His wolf was dominant enough to do so. One day they'd probably brawl to see who was more powerful. Not this evening, when regular humans could get hurt, however. "I didn't know you were in town."

A muscle in Arek's jaw visibly tightened. "If you'd picked up your phone, you'd know," he growled.

Magnus's wolf rose in response to the anger permeating the air. He faked calm, even though he knew Arek would notice his beast. "Right."

Arek glared at him for a few beats. His eyes lightened to the icy-blue color of his wolf's gaze. "Don't fuck with me. I'm in no mood for games."

Fury drove Magnus's beast even closer to the surface. His eyes would now be yellow, and he aimed that sulfur-colored gaze at Arek. "Games?" he breathed out in a low growl. "*I'm* playing games?" He laughed bitterly. "You are the one who likes political bullshit. I refused all that when I declined the alpha role in my old pack." He tilted his head, still locking gazes with Arek.

The shifter returned the stare. "True, but remaining rogue is now impossible."

Magnus sighed. "I've heard that before, remember?" The packs of the United States had during the last two decades formed larger coalitions. There were four Commanding Alphas. Arek actually cared about his packs, but Magnus had a healthy distrust of authority. He'd once sworn fealty to an alpha, which turned out to be a disastrous decision.

Suddenly, his wolf clamored for attention, and he looked around the room for the source of the beast's agitation.

Jasmina Parker stood at the bar, dressed in a short red dress that hugged her delectable curves in all the right places. Her sculpted legs went on for miles before ending in a pair of strappy heels that made his mouth water. The overhead spotlights revealed red highlights in her shoulder-length light brown hair.

"I know you want to remain unpledged due to your...bad experience." Arek relaxed and his eyes returned to their usual deep blue.

"That's one way of describing it." Magnus would characterize it as being tortured by a deranged sadistic alpha, but he'd lost the thread of the conversation because his wolf wanted—needed—to go see Jasmina.

Arek cleared his throat. "You've been rogue for decades now. It's not good for your wolf. You need pack ties to help calm him. I can see that he is almost controlling you."

He was right. The wolf was on high alert, but that was all Jasmina's fault. A hundred pack mates singing lullabies would not calm the beast with her in the room. He'd been obsessed with her from day one, but she'd turned away from him each time. However, he could sense her interest, and it was time to let his wolf have free rein. Magnus pushed the glass of now warm champagne to the center of the table. "Talk to you later," he said.

Arek grabbed his jacket sleeve before he could leave. "We are on the precipice of major changes. Dangerous changes. You cannot ignore this." Magnus snarled, but Arek held on. "There are other things we have to discuss. Did you know that Odin and Freya sent immortal *einherjar* to Midgard? Loki's been sending hybrid monsters to this realm and the immortal Vikings are here to defeat them."

Magnus shook lose from the other wolf's grip. "Yeah. I've seen them. I didn't know that's what they are, but I helped one of them defeat some weird wolverine hybrids a while back."

"You've met them?" Arek sputtered.

Magnus took a breath and sighed inwardly. He shouldn't have shared that information. Now he'd never get out of this conversation. "We'll have breakfast tomorrow." He had to eat anyway. Discussing pack politics and whatever these *einherjar* were would suck, but agreeing to talk tomorrow would get him quicker to where he needed to be now.

Next to the woman in the red dress.

CHAPTER 2

Mina waited for the bartender to mix her gin and tonic. She needed fortification for the tedious evening ahead. Her new position at the magazine's Lifestyle section meant she now wrote fluff pieces about Denver's rich and beautiful instead of the hard-core investigative pieces she'd been hired to do. All because she'd been put in an impossible situation and refused to compromise her ethics.

Technically, she didn't even have to attend this event to write about it. She had a copy of the guest list and the organizer had promised to email her the auction results. The magazine's photographer would take care of the visuals for the piece. But her editor believed in giving the readers an "in the moment" experience. So here Mina was, eavesdropping on the rich and entitled so she could pepper the article with gossip.

The bartender finally finished making her drink. She was about to start mingling when a sizzle of awareness trailed down her spine.

Only one man ever caused that reaction. As if she'd conjured him out of her hot dreams, there he was. Self-made billionaire Magnus Flink. CEO of Dold, the most high-earning software security company in the United States, and voted Denver's most eligible bachelor.

But it wasn't his square chin, sexy dimples, taut body, or vast fortune that made him haunt her dreams. It was the aura of danger that clung to him. She'd always been a sucker for bad boys, and *this* bad boy in *that* tux had her hormones salivating.

Too bad he was the reason she now wrote articles that made her search the thesaurus for adjectives to describe rich people's outfits.

"Jasmina Parker." His deep tone did funny things to her insides, but she ignored that. At least she tried to. Flink ordered a beer and then aimed his emerald green gaze on her. "On assignment for another riveting piece about our city's elite?"

She pasted a fake sunny smile on her lips. "I've told you before that I prefer Mina, but yes, I am. What kind of art does Denver's most eligible bachelor prefer?"

His face clouded over as he grabbed the beer from the bartender and tipped generously. Flink had been grouchy the whole time she'd interviewed him for the bachelor article. If the contest hadn't been to raise money for a homeless shelter, she doubted he'd have participated.

After that interview, she'd run into him at a few events. She always reacted with this hot, sizzling, instant sexual attraction that made her body hum in pleasure. The worst part was with a shifter's power of scent, he knew his effect on her.

And that was the crux of the problem. Mina *knew* he hid a wolf inside him, and she'd nearly been killed by one of his kind. No matter how sexy Flink was, she'd never put herself in that position again.

The eligible bachelor interview had been for a good cause, but it had also been a cover to get close to Flink. Her editor wanted an in-depth article about how the billionaire had built his company and massive fortune. And she did find out, but had she written that he had been alive in the early days of computers—and yes, even when the term referred to humans doing calculations—her editor would have demanded she take a few weeks off, maybe years.

She'd dated a guy in college who hid a wolf inside him. When Flink's eyes had turned yellow because the photographer wanted yet another pose, she'd recognized him as a shifter, and the danger he posed to her.

Flink turned toward her now, a polite smile on his lips. "My tastes? I like all beautiful creations." Although his gaze never left hers, her nerve endings told her he slowly perused her body all the way down and then up again.

Her nipples tightened in response, or maybe that was just because he stood so close his body heat enfolded her. A blush heated her cheeks, and she looked down, fiddling with the straw in her glass. "I'm sure you'll find many examples of beauty here tonight. Although many of the people have expressions as stiff as the portraits on the wall, because of Botox."

His smile deepened into something more genuine. He cupped Mina's elbow, steering her toward a table in the corner. Two other men were also heading that way, but a look from Flink had them quickly changing direction. "Seriously, why are you writing about high society?"

Mina put her drink on the table and next to it, placed her small evening purse. "I write about whatever my editor assigns me."

He positioned himself with his back toward the wall, and yet his body sheltered her from the crowd. "Your editor is an idiot. I've read some of your articles."

She ignored the warmth spreading through her body at his unintentional compliment. "You googled me?"

He leaned forward, elbows on the table. "I research everyone writing about me." Foolish her for thinking she was special. "What happened that made your assignments change?"

Mina thought about giving the official spiel about new career opportunities and challenges, but her feet already hurt in the ridiculous high strappy sandals she'd chosen to wear.

For him. In case he'd be here.

Her hormones made her do it, and she couldn't hide her reaction any longer. It was obvious he knew she was attracted to him, so she might as well give him the truth and tell him to get lost. She lifted one leg and rotated her foot to relieve her squashed toes. "You happened."

"I caused your demotion?" His eyebrows rose.

"My editor wanted to find out why you are leagues ahead of your competitors, both in technology and earnings. He suspects something illegal."

Flink shook his head. "He demoted you when you told him my success is due to only hard work and determination?"

"Oh no, I found the real reason for your prosperity." She sucked down the rest of her drink. "You have personal knowledge of all historical computer research. Of course, nobody would believe me if I wrote that. I refuse to report lies, so I had to refuse the assignment."

Flink laughed. "Personal knowledge? You think I'm immortal?"

"No, but wolf shifters live a very long time."

"I'm a werewolf?" His voice lowered, and his eyes shifted from green to honey-color. His wolf observed her now. "Aren't you a little too old for fairy tales?"

Even people who didn't know shifters walked among them would instinctively flee from that yellow gaze. But she'd battled one big bad wolf already, so she leaned closer. "You can growl your denial all you want, but when your eyes turn yellow, I see the beast inside you."

His eyebrows rose, and then he smiled. "Come home with me."

Her body screamed yes. She ignored it. "I prefer to know my lovers on an emotional level before we have sex."

He tilted his head. A very wolf-like gesture. "Does emotional closeness always have to proceed physical intimacy? Could a relationship not start the other way around?"

"Does that line ever work?"

"You tell me. I've never tried it on anyone else." His eyes were back to emerald green.

Mina believed him, and she actually had no problem with causal sex. However, in this case, fantasizing about how hot the two of them would be together would have to be enough.

Her ex-boyfriend had turned obsessively jealous and had for days physically restrained her to stop her from leaving his house. He couldn't help it, because his wolf had decided she was its mate. Dating a shifter was not an experience she would repeat.

"I've had a long day and am too tired for this game. Have a pleasant evening." She picked up her bag and walked toward the exit.

CHAPTER 3

After the cold air conditioning inside the museum's lobby, Mina relished the warm summer night air that caressed her bare shoulders. The weather report had promised a balmy evening, so she hadn't bothered with a coat. The way the close proximity to one hot wolf in a killer tuxedo had overheated her body, she wouldn't have needed one even if the season had been an extra frigid Colorado winter. She took out her phone and opened the ride-share app.

Fast steps behind her had her turning around quickly with her breath held.

Flink slowed his steps as he got closer and grabbed her hand. "I don't want to part on bad terms." His callused palm felt warm against hers.

"We didn't." She resumed breathing and tried to free herself.

He held on. "Give me a few moments." He stepped off the curb and tugged her with him. "I need to—"

The loud laugher of a group leaving the event interrupted him.

He pulled her with him as he stepped into a narrow alley between two buildings. The light from the glass walls of the lobby barely reached into the shadows but illuminated his face enough to where she could see his serious expression. "We need to talk."

Mina shook her head. "I don't think that is a good idea." She tugged on her hand again. This time he let go, but she didn't leave. She stood there, waiting for something, but she didn't know what.

"If you won't listen to words, maybe this will get your attention." He bracketed her face with his palms. "I've been wanting to do this for months," he whispered as he leaned in and captured her lips with his.

Mina closed her eyes and savored the kiss she'd pictured in her mind so many times. His firm lips slowly explored hers. She leaned into him. This was madness, but she'd been wondering for months what this would be like.

He tilted his head and increased the pressure of the kiss, demanding more access.

When she yielded, he groaned, and his tongue thrust into her mouth.

Her body ignited, and she pressed closer.

A moan escaped her as his hands slid down her back, pushing so that her heat met his hardness. Mina tugged on the collar of his shirt. She needed more.

She needed *him*.

Her nipples brushed against the structured fabric of his jacket, sending sizzles of pleasure straight to her core. Her eyes flew open, and she struggled to catch her breath. "This is crazy. We're outside. Anyone could see us."

She lost interest in their location when he buried his hands in her hair, tilting her head to deepen the kiss, and then those clever lips traced kisses along her jaw and down her neck. She sighed with pleasure and closed her eyes again as he went lower and sucked on her collarbone.

"More," she murmured, pulling on his collar again, but Flink resisted—a little too much. She opened her eyes and leaned back. His jaw clenched, but his body remained as still as a marble statue. "What's going on?"

His eyes turned honey-colored and focused on something behind her. A low growl rumbled in his throat.

Arms of steel grabbed her from behind, banded around her middle and neck, and pressed her against a hard chest. "This is a sweet treat," an accented voice said. She couldn't tell if it was Russian or Eastern European. "I may have a little taste myself before I hand her over to the boss."

Anger distorted Magnus' face, and a muscle pulsed in his jaw, but his body remained frozen.

Mina fought against the man. His grip wouldn't budge. Instead, he increased the pressure around her neck, forcing her chin up as she struggled for breath.

Helpless, she stared at Magnus, whose eyes glared at her captor.

The man dragged her deeper into the alley. Mina relaxed all her muscles, but becoming deadweight just increased the pressure against her throat, cutting off her oxygen.

He dragged her around the building to a car parked beneath an overhang. When he had to use the arm holding her around her waist to open the door, she fought with all her might, scratching his arm and kicking his shin.

She stomped her heel on his instep.

The attacker shouted in a foreign language but renewed his grip around her waist so roughly that she lost her footing. She went down in a heap on the ground, dragging the man with her. The asphalt scraped the skin on her bare legs, but Mina ignored the pain and scrambled, trying to get away. She felt the man's fingers in her hair, pulling hard, and then slamming her head into the pavement.

Everything went black.

CHAPTER 4

Four hundred and eighty seconds.

Eight fucking minutes.

That's how long it took for whatever had frozen Magnus to lose its hold. He'd been counting every tick of the Breguet watch on his wrist. By the time he'd run down the alley to where the shifter had dragged Jasmina, they were long gone. There wasn't even a scent trail to follow.

He raked his hand through his hair. There had been a thud and Jasmina's screams had cut off. If that fucker had hurt her... he had to swallow the bile that rose in his throat.

How had the bastard cloaked himself from Magnus's senses? And what in the hell had he used to freeze him? He'd lost complete control of his muscles and could only watch as the fucker dragged Jasmina, *his* Mina, down the alley.

If the shifter used some kind of paralyzing agent, Magnus couldn't risk Mina's safety by going after him alone. Backup was needed. Grabbing his phone, he dialed the number that was listed several times in his recent calls log.

Arek answered on the third ring. "A little early for breakfast. I haven't even gone to bed yet." Loud music played in the background.

"I need your help," Magnus bit out. "I'm outside the Museum of Art." He hung up before Arek wasted time by asking questions.

Pacing the alley, he again counted seconds. His wolf wanted them to shift so they could go hunting, but without a trail, there was no use. Why had the Russian wolf targeted Mina? She knew something about the shifter world, but he doubted a regular human would be involved in pack politics.

After five hundred and ninety-two seconds, Arek finally arrived. "I was at a bar on the other side of downtown. They had a really good band—"

"No time for chit chat," Magnus growled.

Arek's eyes lightened, but he asked in a calm voice, "What happened?"

Magnus described Mina's abduction.

"Russian accent," Arek said. "That could be one of Novikov's wolfs."

"The second of the New York pack?" Magnus shook his head. "Why would he kidnap Mina?"

The other shifter sighed. "This is why I am here. Novikov challenged his alpha last year and won. He's now the commanding alpha of the Eastern Packs, and he has ambitions to expand into the Midwest."

"The alpha in charge of the central regions is one of the strongest wolves alive. Novikov can't defeat him."

"With the help of his new wife he can," Arek answered. "He's married a dark witch."

"Fuck." Magic fueled by blood sacrifices had rendered him immobile. His former alpha had dabbled in that shit. "Why would he take Mina?" He paced again.

"Because you were with her." Arek sat down on one of the couches. "This is what I've been trying to talk to you about. Novikov is about to start, if not a war, a major conflict. He's going to use your woman to pressure you into joining his pack."

"And thereby force me to pay him tithing." Each pack member paid a percentage of their income to the pack. The money was supposedly for expenses like those of the full moon hunt, but some packs purchased weapons and fortifications.

"Exactly," Arek answered. "With your wealth and his wife's skills, he'll be able to take over a good chunk of the US, if not all of it."

Magnus would pay anything to get Mina back, but handing over money to someone that resorted to kidnapping did not give him confidence that they would return her unhurt, or at all. "We have to find them before they leave Denver." He looked at Arek's medallion. "Can you use your magic jewelry?"

The other shifter's lips stretched into a wry smile. "Don't tell me you believe those stupid rumors." He grasped the medallion. "This was my grandfather's. It works as a focus to tap into the mental connections I have with my pack, but only because it has value to me. It is worth nothing in monetary terms." He put his hand on Magnus's arm. "I doubt Novikov's wolf will drive all the way back to New York. He probably has a private plane waiting somewhere."

Magnus walked toward the museum parking lot. "The metropolitan area of Denver has four municipal airports. Five if we count Boulder." He patted his pockets for the keys to his Tesla Model S. "Centennial is south of here, but all the others are north, so let's head that way."

Suddenly, his wolf gave alert for—not danger exactly—but it insisted on taking over his senses the way it did when they were hunting. Magnus had learned the hard way to pay attention to his wolf, and this was something new. He stopped.

Arek, who'd been following closely, almost smacked in to him. "What's going on?"

"I don't know. The wolf is trying to tell me something." He closed his eyes. "It's like when it has picked up a scent trail, but it is not quite that."

"Are you bonded to your woman?" the older wolf asked.

"She's not exactly my woman," Magnus said. "The wolf has decided he wants her, that's all." Although he had kissed her. Touched her.

"Maybe he can find her."

Magnus tossed him the key fob. "You drive, and I'll concentrate on whatever the wolf is trying to tell me."

Arek grinned when he saw what car unlocked when he pressed the button. "I've always wanted to drive one of these."

Magnus' beast sent images and impressions so quickly he couldn't keep up. He slid into the passenger seat. The double vision of the road that the Tesla traveled on, and the journey the wolf seemed to be on, made him close his eyes. The beast became more agitated.

"I'm just heading north on I-25 and hope you'll tell me if, or when, I have to exit," Arek said.

Magnus' wolf provided scents, sounds, and images through their connection. But it wasn't anything Magnus could translate into driving directions.

The wolf told him they'd once chased a bunny across soft grass nearby Mina's current location, but Magnus had run in wolf form in most of Denver's urban green areas and the surrounding beautiful wilderness.

Finally, the beast sent something that made sense. A store that made wooden furniture that smelled like actual trees.

"They're heading for Erie Airport." Magnus gave Arek directions. Thank goodness he'd shopped for a custom-made barn door a few weeks ago.

The alpha pressed down on the gas pedal, and twenty minutes later, they reached the small municipal airport north of Denver. Dawn lightened the sky in the west as they parked half a mile from the official lot.

Both of them shifted to wolf. Being fully one with his animal freed something inside Magnus. Feelings not his own flooded his senses.

Mina's feelings.

She was angry—no, furious.

He took lead as they ran toward a small jet on the runway that looked ready to take off. Sounds of struggle came from inside the plane.

They were still fifty yards away from the aircraft when a muffled banging erupted, and the door flew open, revealing Mina tumbling to the ground and landing in a controlled tuck-and-roll. She immediately slid into the shadows under the body of the plane.

The Russian jumped down after her. His feet had barely touched the ground before Magnus tackled him and sank his teeth into the man's throat.

Blood splattered the side of the plane as he tore open a carotid artery, but he didn't care. It was a just killing.

The man had taken his Mina. He struggled to not completely lose himself to the wolf's blood lust. During the full moon hunt, he let the wolf celebrate the take-down of prey by feasting on the meat. But this was not venison.

He struggled to control the beast. It protested, so Magnus sent it an image of Mina.

Protect your mate.

The wolf immediately stood down and looked for her.

Mina appeared from underneath the plane and crouched on the ground, one hand stretched out toward them.

"It's okay," she said. "I'm fine. You can shift back now." She looked cautiously toward Arek, who stood to the side, intently focused on Mina. "I'm just going to trust that this is a buddy of yours." She slid closer to Magnus. In his wolf form, he was the size of a small pony. "You're beautiful." She touched the fur on his neck. "You saved me."

A feeling of peace flooded his senses as her fingers brushed his pelt and he changed back to his human form.

He buried his nose in her hair. Her scent calmed him further. "Trust me. Just a little."

She sighed. "How can I not?"

Mine, his wolf growled.

Ours, Magnus corrected, and the beast reluctantly agreed.

EPILOGUE

Six months later.

Mina closed her laptop and stretched to work out the kinks in her neck. She'd just emailed her report to another satisfied client. Setting out on her own had been hard at first, but Arek had been an enormous help. He ran a physical security firm—as opposed to Magnus' software security—and Mina's investigative skills had proven themselves a great asset to his business. She helped vet clients and also to track down adversaries that could be the threat that caused some of them to hire Arek in the first place.

She walked out of the spare bedroom that served as her office. The floor-to-ceiling windows facing west showed brilliant blue sky over the snowcapped Rocky Mountains. She'd feel bad about living in this luxurious abode on the top floor of the Four Seasons Private Residences, but her new business earned well, and she liked the secure location. It would be hard for stray wolves, even with the help of dark magic, to reach them here.

Her working with Arek had given Magnus a "consultant to the Pacific Packs" status. He was not a full member, but the ties were close enough to where other alphas had stopped pursuing him.

And she'd come to terms with dating a wolf and working with wolves. Her ex hadn't been a jealous possessive jerk because he was a shifter. He'd been a regular controlling asshole who happened to hide a wolf inside.

"There you are," Magnus said when she reached the living room. He rose from one of the cream-colored couches. His hair stood up on end as if he'd run his fingers through it.

"Is something wrong?"

He took a step toward her but then stopped. Retrieving a small box from his pocket, he kneeled down on one knee. "Mina, marry me." As usual, he made a demand out of what should be a question.

She stared down into the opened box. A big Asscher cut canary diamond surrounded by smaller round-cut white diamonds sparkled in the sunlight. "It's the color of your wolf's eyes."

"That's not an answer."

"There was a question?" She placed the exquisite ring on her finger and stretched her arm out. "It reminds me of a daisy."

"Mina," her fiancé growled.

"Yes," she said and leaned down to kiss her wolf.

Do you want more of the *Norse Warrior Protectors*? The first book in the series is *Berserker Obsession*. All the books are listed here: https://www.asamariabradley.com/norsewarriorprotectors/.

The ebooks are available on Amazon and in Kindle Unlimited and you can find the print versions wherever books are sold.

If you haven't already, subscribe to my newsletter for new releases updates, bonus content, and exclusive giveaways: www.asamariabradley.com/newsletter/

Thank you for reading my stories!

ABOUT ASA MARIA BRADLEY

USA Today bestselling author Asa Maria Bradley grew up in Sweden surrounded by archaeology and history steeped in Norse mythology, which inspired her sexy paranormal romance and sizzling urban fantasy series.

Booklist attributes her writing with "nonstop action, satisfying romantic encounters, and intriguing world building" and *Entertainment Weekly* says "when it comes to paranormal romance with explosive action scenes, Bradley has that nailed." Her work has received the honors of a double nomination for the Romance Writers of America's RITA contest, a Reviewers' Choice Award nomination, a Holt Medallion win, and a Booksellers' Best Award win.

Asa came to the United States as a high school exchange student and quickly fell in love with ranch dressing and crime TV dramas of all flavors, two addictions she unfortunately still struggles with. Currently, she lives on a lake deep in the forest of the Pacific Northwest with a British husband and a rescue dog of indeterminate breed. Sadly, neither of them obeys her commands.

Sign up for her newsletter for new releases updates, bonus content, and exclusive giveaways: www.asamariabradley.com/newsletter.

facebook.com/AsaMariaBradley.Author

x.com/AsaMariaBradley

instagram.com/asamariabradley

amazon.com/author/asamariabradley

bookbub.com/authors/asa-maria-bradley

goodreads.com/asamariabradley

tiktok.com/@asamariabradley

ALSO BY ASA MARIA BRADLEY

For the most current list, please visit

www.AsaMariaBradley.com/books.

The *Norse Warrior Protectors* Series

Wolf Desire Short Story (Magnus & Mina)

Berserker Obsession (Leif & Naya)

Berserker Temptation (Luke & Astrid)

Wolf Hunger (Arek & Laney)

Berserker Devotion (Ulf & Nora)

Wolf Promise (Bolt & Regie)

The *Powers of Lightning* Series

(Urban Fantasy/Supernatural Suspense)

Flash of Fear

Flash of Fate

***A Grifter's Song* Multi-Author Series**

(Crime Fiction)

Upgrade

Made in United States
Troutdale, OR
08/10/2024